PUNK ROCKER

Presented by
Brenda Perlin

Blossoming Press

Published by arrangement with Blossoming Press

Copyright © 2016 by Brenda Perlin

Copyright for each story is held by the individual authors and/or publishers.

Burn Zone excerpts reprinted with permission: Jorge P. Newbery; Community Books, L.L.C.

All rights reserved. No part of this publication may be reproduced or transmitted in any form or by any means, electronic or mechanical, including photocopying, recording, or by any information storage and retrieval system, without permission in writing from the author.

This is a work of fiction. Any resemblance of characters to actual persons, living or dead, is purely coincidental.

ISBN-13:978-1523806676
ISBN-10:1523806672

Cover design by Steven Novak

Photographs © Brenda Perlin | BlossomingPress.com

Acknowledgements

This is for all the young punks who were as misunderstood as I was.

Thank you to the people who have shared their stories in Punk Rocker and to my friends who were by my side during this time period.

Gratitude to KS Brooks and Stephen Hise of Indies Unlimited. Their support of authors is beyond measure.

MAB, my Spartan warrior princess, works tirelessly on all of my projects with grace and finesse. She goes far and beyond to help me no matter what the subject matter happens to be.

Mark Barry pulled these stories out of me. He gave me the motivation and enthusiasm to go back to my punk days. Something I wasn't sure I wanted to do. He has made this more fun for me than I could have imagined.

Many thanks to the BILLY IDOL Female Fans Worldwide #BIFFWW for their friendship and support.

To Ron, my significant other and best friend. He has more than tolerated the endless Billy Idol, Scott Weiland and David Bowie talk. He is my prince!

All my books are dedicated to my love of reading, enhanced greatly after I discovered the hypnotic writing of Pat Conroy.

© Brenda Perlin | BlossomingPress.com

David Bowie
The Thin White Duke 76
Picture Credit: Wikimedia Commons

David Bowie
A Dedication
by
Brenda Perlin

I wake up this icy January morning to see the unimaginable: The words #RIP David Bowie typed all over my social media.

My heart deflates. All I could think was ... oh no!!!! Not Bowie. Not him. No. Not yet. We are not ready to lose him. To me – and all those who loved him – David Bowie was immortal. He was supposed to grow old gracefully and with style. He would have, too. A hundred-year-old Bowie would have been brilliant. Still not conforming. Standing out in a way only The Thin White Duke could.

I thought back to one stellar point in time. Summer 1983. We had just made it backstage at the US Festival in San Bernardino. Susie, my best friend, had a sister with connections in the music business and generously, she shared backstage passes with us. We didn't have to be away from the action, crowded amongst sweaty fans and caked in mud while burning in the summer heat. We were the lucky ones.

As we made our way around the band's trailers, we spotted a small commotion to our right. Being star-struck teenagers, we needed to discover what the fuss was all about and, thankfully, we did. Within seconds, there we stood. Right. Next. To. David. Bowie. To most, he was an icon. To us, he was OUR hero. I wasn't even able to get a word out because I looked into those mismatched eyes, and thought this is a day I will never forget. This is me making history. I didn't do or say anything, but I didn't have to: My hero crossed my path, and I would never be the same again.

Shortly after, the man took the stage, and there we were, watching Bowie in action. Doing his thing like no one else in the world could. As he sang songs such as

Star, Heroes, Golden Years, Fashion, and loads of his other greatest hits, with the music belting from the speakers, I had goose bumps all over my body.

After seeing him on MTV, television programs and movies, to get a glimpse of him in the flesh practically put me in shock! My emotions must have been the same ones fans had when they saw the Beatles in the sixties. It was electrifying.

A legend was commanding the stage. Standing dead center. With his platinum rockabilly hairstyle, donning a glam pink suit with shoulder pads to the max, he stood there like a God from another planet. In that moment, I believed anything was possible. For me, that afternoon was a life-changer. He made it okay to be direct. To be different. To stand out on your own and to shine no matter what. He personified what punk rock represents. He was no follower, not a preacher, never boring, but a true artist in every sense of the word.

Spaceman, may you always shine bright and bring life to Mars the way you have to Earth.

Scott Weiland
Live at Pepsi Music Stadium April 16, 2007
Picture Credit: Wikimedia Commons

Scott Weiland
A Dedication
by
Jim Kavanagh

Late morning, December 4, 2015.

After my early morning coffee and train commute into New York City, I sat in a corner office of the Empire State Building. A magnificent southern view with the sunrise beginning to cast a beautiful light over downtown Manhattan.

An associate stuck his head into my office and said, "Did you see Scott Weiland at the Paramount Sunday? Well, he was found dead this morning."

My first reaction was disbelief as I surfed through the news on my iPhone. I wasn't convinced that this story was true and suspected it could be a hoax. As most of us have experienced, these mistakes are insanely common in this world of handheld information technology. I had been duped in the past, and before I let this wave of emotion and loss totally engulf me, I had better be sure.

I was on a five-week safari out in the bush with local natives in South Africa Christmas of 2013. Besides my tattoos, they loved everything to do with Americana Rap music. (Not my genre, and not music I have listened to outside of telling my kids to turn the crap down ... I've become my Father.) Anyway...

I was the only one with a phone sophisticated enough to retrieve any kind of Internet signal. I was able to access the Internet every day while driving on a remote dirt road entering Kruger National Park. ... so, with three days left to my trip, there was a notice on my phone that the rapper 50 Cent had been killed in a violent drive-by shooting. Stunned, I shared this news with my native friends, only to experience long faces, tears and hearing track-after-track of 50 Cent songs for the remainder of my stay. I felt horrible being the bearer of such bad news. These people were so connected to his music that it moved me to watch them, and listen to their experiences and introduction to his music. I was perplexed that 50 Cent music touched all of these people in the wilds of Africa. We were a body short of having a real wake, although I was honestly stunned at their appreciation and affection this music gave them.

I could not help but reflect and consider my connection to music. Artists like Bon Scott, John Bonham, Sid Vicious, Layne Staley, and, of course, John Lennon. Their passing bothered me immensely for different reasons.

While walking through the airport at the end of my trip, I was on the phone with one of my sons, checking on things at home when I began sharing with him the deep emotional bond created in South Africa over 50 Cent's death. Imagine, for a moment, my surprise after his laughter finally subsided, when he told me that 50 Cent was alive and well. It was all a hoax. Never was I so ashamed. Every conversation after that felt like I had to pull the foreskin down over my dickhead just to speak. Long flight home to say the least!

I still don't know why I cried the way I did after finding out that Scott Weiland did, indeed, pass away. At fifty-three, I often feel my youth has quickly slipped away. Discovering Stone Temple Pilots in my thirties, I fell into a sound that I didn't think was possible at that stage of my life. A sound that made me want to rock, dance, sing and swing my head around like I did as a punk teenager listening to a young Billy Idol utter the words "Ready, Steady, Go"...

Over the next twenty-four years or so, I saw Scott Weiland and his different band mates about a dozen times. I met him, laughed with him, and had a beer with him. I adored him and his words, and now that he's gone, they somehow mean more to me. I mourn because, selfishly, I can't see him anymore and am no longer able to act and feel young again at one of his shows. To gaze in amazement at his moves and sound. The ultimate front-man.

I bury my head on that rock altar again. I don't say goodbye, after all, we still have his music. I ponder the mysterious question of "why"? I don't care for anyone's speculation, conjecture or scientific reasoning as to how ... I'm a living witness to his performances on stage and his warm personality off stage.

I won't be spared these feelings of loss and sorrow. But, I won't look into the shadows! I will look into the light and pump my fist in the air!

License to Thrill
Carla Mullins
© 2016

Carla Mullins is a thirty-five year old housewife residing in London whose hobbies include writing poetry and a love affair with punk rock.

He's the original rebel
the real thing;
your soul is touched when you hear him sing.

He's lived a wild life, it's true to say,
he's like a god, still here large today.

Like a magnet he's drawn you in;
once you're hooked, that's it;
you don't want to stop loving him.

Such a legend of huge fame,
the punkrocker puts others to shame.

Unstoppable force he sure is,
it's an addiction, and you need the fix.

He set out decades ago to shine;
his dream came true,
and he's still oh, so fine.

That voice of his gives me shivers, you see.
For I will never not adore,
that man is meant to be.

"We wanted change. It wasn't about breaking the rules. It was about breaking barriers."

Jim Kavanagh – NYC Punk

Image by Silvano L. Marlon
© Brenda Perlin | BlossomingPress.com

Highway One
A Fictional Billy Idol Tale
Mark Barry
© 2016

Mark Barry is an English writer and music fan who has written several novels, including the award-winning The Night Porter. The short stories, King Rocker and One Night In Richmond Park, are featured in the L.A. Punk Rocker anthology. Mark currently resides in Nottingham, England.

The Pacific Ocean is unimaginably vast and today, it acts as a mirror to the sky – a daunting expanse of unsullied aquamarine-tinted silvered glass.

When Billy was at school all those years ago, a balding, stinky-jacketed geography teacher whose name he forgot the minute he left the school gates for good, informed them that the Pacific constituted over half the surface area of the globe. Looking at it now, from a clifftop just north of Bodega Bay on a late summer's day, he can see exactly what he meant.

It is endless.

It's more than half the world, he thinks. Way more than half.

Nothing obscured Billy's view. No piers or ramshackles, no wrecks, canoes, schooners, liners or pleasure boats. No blotches of black seaweed. Hard to believe how ancient mariners would dare to set sail with this enormous expanse of sapphire and waves before them. In those days where the horizon was the feared tipping point, dragons and krakens sank the wary, the stray and the lost and those that survived then fell off the precipice into the void. Those sailors had guts: Drake was the first European to set foot on this coast, and he was the bravest – and most insane – of them all, Billy considers, as a light breeze blows a stray leaf past his buckled boot.

A half-starved gull squawks. He's been standing there for ten minutes sipping Evian from his supplies bag. Ready, he stretches his legs and throws his arms wide to loosen the pecs and make supple the elbows and shoulders.

Behind him, the Harley. It calls him now.

Long old way to go, matey, he sighs, and turns away from the ocean, a gesture, which strikes him as simultaneously impolite and essential.

It's a hot, hot day on the coast of California. In his mind's ear, he hears Lou Reed. His mental radio has been tuned into him all day. At that precise point in time, at that nexus in existence, Billy reflects that he wouldn't be anywhere else. Running his fingers through his still-platinum spikes, he puts on his full-face helmet with a ghostly black visor that snaps into place perfectly, connecting with a satisfying click of totality. The screen obscures his face. He is temporarily depersonalised by it, freed. He could be anyone.

Freedom.

Just him, the iconic punk rock star Billy Idol, his beloved Harley, all chrome and tube with Ghost Rider wheels ready to blaze.

And Highway One, all 630 miles of it.

He is biking as far north as he can go. Billy loves his motorcycle and the road, this metaphysical, divine combination. He's on the third day of an odyssey, with, like Chuck Berry, no particular place to go. In another week, the Idol colossus goes on tour and this sense of peace and freedom will be replaced by a frenzy of chaos and crashing power chords. It's a massive nationwide tour. A sell-out. Not a ticket to be had on the web. Record multiples on eBay and the parasite portals: Meet and Greet packages in Vegas changing hands for the price of a family motor. They're coming over from Britain and Australia in their hundreds, like Cabot and Drake and Raleigh and Frobisher; something that fills him with pride whenever he ponders on it.

His legions.

Billy "King Rocker" Idol at sixty.

Like the Shooting Star, he has been doing this for forty years plus – if you count the days he followed the Pistols round the Shires of England in the early days of the punk revolution. He knows that he will have to store away the Harley (and the Triumph at home). His soul empties whenever the reality of being without his bike enters his head. He wishes he could ride to each gig, but the maw of America would swallow him whole. He knows it.

As he ambles back to the bike, he notices someone near the Harley. The shape is sitting on the wall facing the road. Closer, he sees the shape is a girl. Long dark hair, a black leather biker jacket (a bit like his). A small light blue rucksack hanging from her shoulder. She's looking north as if waiting for someone to arrive. Billy didn't notice her when he pulled into to the picnic area. He imagines she must have been dropped off by a car or a truck, but why here? This place is miles away from the next town. He gets on his bike, embraces the wraithlike, trembling rumble between his thighs, like a chrome-and-ebon racehorse in the stalls, and creeps towards her. Parallel, he lifts up his visor.
Okay, love? Billy asks.
I need a ride, she replies, matter of fact.
Billy is inclined to say no, but he is first and foremost an Englishman and this woman; early twenties, with her First Nation colouring and impossibly deep brown eyes, all encased in a faceful of attitude, is in need of assistance. In the end, there is nothing he can do. It's in the programming.
That's cool. Where are you going?
She answers a question with a question.

Are you English?

Yeh. Live here though. LA. Have done for years.

Awesome, she responds enigmatically. Heading up to Oregon, but I'll take whatever miles you have to offer.

How does Crescent City sound? Seeing friends up there tomorrow. It's about three hundred miles. Six or seven hours if we take time to enjoy the view, yeh. Happy with that?

Totally, she says. Appreciate it.

I've got a spare helmet. Hang on. Can you ride?

Been riding horses since I was a kid. Bikes are no problem, she says, the merest hint of a smile on her face (but only a hint).

Climb aboard, love, Billy says.

English, she whispers to herself. Looks at the helmet she has been given with unfathomable inscrutability.

William, he offers, along with his hand. If she recognises him, she says nothing. He's not going to enlighten her. Let's see what she does, he thinks, which is a conceit, but an altogether understandable one.

Francesca. Call me Fran, she says, climbing aboard.

Though his helmet muffles the senses, he can smell cigarettes, perfume, cinnamon, wood smoke and something he can't place, something unusual. He has an immediate flashback to London, in the nineties. Someone he met at a gig, or maybe in LA, someone he met in rehab – his memory is not what it was. He waits for her to put on her helmet. She tucks into him, but holds the pillion bar on the back, so her connection to the bike is made with her jeans clamping his hips in that strange pseudo-intimacy only bikers can truly appreciate.

Rock n' roll, Billy thinks and sweeps majestically on to the road to Crescent City.

Highway One.

Billy loves biking here. Saturday, Sundays especially, and when he can, long trips like this one, staying in cheap motels, filling up in Mom and Pop diners. Relaxation – not of the body, but of the mind and the spirit. It isn't desert (a place you can genuinely find yourself), but at the right time, and staying out of the city itself, he finds the peace and solitude he needs to rewind the batteries. He loves the sea, and the cliffsides and the greenery and the trees and the cloudless, rolling sky. They started building this, he knows, in 1922, and they kept on building it and building it bit-by-bit until it was said that the highway would never stop until it reached the stars. They built it with picks and shovels and bloody hands and the road builders died in their hundreds in a world where life was cheap. Where mountains stood in the way of the roadbuilders they blasted their way through with TNT and gelignite and old gunpowder salvaged from unused grenades from WW1. They built bridges like the Bixby Bridge in Big Sur to span canyons and ravines with no conceivable nadir except the Hell at the climax of their existence.

Billy loves this history, even if a tiny part of him reflects that his ticket to ride was paid for by the blood, sweat and tears of desperate men. Later, the roadbuilders mechanised (which eradicated the need to use prisoners on twenty cents a day), and that speeded the process and saved lives; the diggers and the cranes, the giant mixers and the black top spreaders, the pneumatic drills and the machine stampers.

They reached Canada faster – but not by much.

Billy and Francesca ride at a steady sixty, the blacktop road is smooth and all around is a sea of emerald grass (though, Billy knows that nothing can ever be as green as the grass back home). Fran says nothing. It is almost as if she isn't there and the hitching sequence at the picnic site was just a dream, a fevered, trippy hallucination. Billy senses she is looking around her, as he is. Curious and open. Billy likes that in a woman. He is partial to intelligent, educated women and something about Fran suggests she is exactly that, adding a hint of the wild. Her nebulous, feminine presence and the tender pressure of her jeaned thighs either side of his hips is the only reminder that he is not alone. They travel together in silence, save for fragments of the sounds of Highway One. The purr of his engine, with potential energy in harness, capable of an explosion at any time, like a lion in the veldt ready to strike. The sound of passing cars, their inhabitants trapped inside mobile metal jails. Roosting birds chirping and calling in the leafy late summer trees, gulls flying inland (a storm in the deep?), and, on one memorable occasion, a giant crimson truck playing Motorhead as Billy overtook the driver's blue check-denimed arm waving him past.

Apart from being on stage, nothing could beat this.
The road.
Nothing.

They drive for a couple of hours with just the sound of tyre on the road and the purr of the engine to keep them company. Billy needs a rest room, and he pulls into a roadside diner just south of Gualala. Parks amidst the cars and the trucks a little bit out of the way.

Fancy something to eat? He asks, as he dismounts the bike and takes off his helmet, puffs up his spikes.

Sure, Francesca says. I'll buy. Thank you.

Wouldn't dream of it, love, Billy says and the two of them head inside, find a booth. It's one of those diners with tiny jukes the size of a shoebox on the table itself. When he returns from the gents, Francesca is pressing the buttons to see what's on. She looks engrossed. Billy wonders whether anything of his will be trapped in the tiny tabletop music box, and if so, will she put two and two together. If there is any Billy on there, when she ceases her surfing, the answer is five.

She's beautiful, he realises – no, beyond that.

Billy has encountered some stellar women out on the road, some women spawned on Planet Unbelievable, and Fran is up there pitching. It's all he can do not to stare. Luckily, he's saved from that drooling fate by a waitress who announces herself as Pearl. They order and make small talk. The service is rapid fire and after a second cup of coffee, Fran raises the conversational stakes.

I've just left Tempus. Know it?

The temptation to grin wryly is overwhelming, but Billy resists it. He takes a sip of his coffee – bitter, too hot. It burns his lip, his famous lip, and he pushes it slightly away from him on the Formica top.

I know Tempus, sure, he replies, somewhat archly.

Billy knows Tempus well, the old Spanish monastery just north of Baja. Inspiring place. Several bracing (and entirely necessary) trips to Tempus helped him say goodbye to the eighties and hello to the (temporarily) clean and sober nineties. But like the mythical Hotel California, Billy knows that you can check out of Tempus, but you can never leave.

Now he spots it. Now she leads him in the right direction, she has the eyes.

Yes.

Tempus eyes. Eyes that know way too much about the world. Eyes that have seen things that should remain mercifully unseen. He knows then that it won't be long before the two of them connect on a level way beyond polite conversation over coffee and eggs on toast.

He wonders why she felt able to bring up the subject.

She must have seen Billy's eyes.

The pair of them, Tempus Fugitives.

The Semper Fi greeting of the rehab world. All for one and one for all.

He wonders. On some level deep in the unconscious, the moment he saw her, did he know, too? He could have driven off.

Sorry, love. I need this isolation.

But he didn't. It was never even an option.

Billy once overdosed so badly on toxic crack, real skanky stuff he scored in Compton one desperate, desperate night, he woke up in Tempus three days later. They had saved his room for him, the kindly souls.

He had been dead for twenty three seconds, but the King Rocker can never truly die.

Three months, she continues. Nice people at Tempus. Saints. All things Columbian put me there mainly, but you know how these things are – you can throw in booze and pills, too, while you're talking. I'm clean now, they told me. Clean and sober and so, on my way I go.

Why Oregon?

Love the country air. Friends up there. They run a nature reserve. Really, it could be anywhere as long as it's away from parties, bars, clubs and bad, bad men. Oregon is as good as anywhere.

Yeh, I've been. Incredible. The trees…

Can you imagine what it was like four hundred years ago when my people only took the trees they needed? The forests must have been everywhere. So awesome. I paint.

You do? Paint?

Francesca laughs and slightly changes the subject. I've got a girlfriend who takes photos of dicks and then paints them.

Billy splurts his coffee on the half eaten bagel. Dicks? Whatever for?

Stripping man back to the basics, she told me. The essence of masculinity in a world run by women. All that's left for men is the dick in their pants according to her, and so, she makes art of it. OMG, she makes serious moolah. Could do with some of that myself.

What? Dick or cash? Billy thinks, mischievously, but he doesn't say it, wouldn't dream of it.

There's a market for dick paintings? He asks instead.

Totally. She's just sold a canvas montage of dicks. Down in Miami.

A montage?

Yep. A collage, like the ones we did at school. Remember? She sold this collage of dicks – white dicks, yellow dicks, black dicks, old man's dicks, tiny dicks, those dicks that get bigger when tickled, those dicks that are longer when they're soft, a collage of all kinds of dicks – for thirty grand.

Thirty large? That's pretty cool, Billy replies.

Yeh. I capture landscapes. I love the trees, and I'm going to paint one of those Sequoias up there. So, what do you do?

Billy is taken aback. He is not used to this.

She really has no idea. In his experience, because of music on TV, most people know Billy Idol. The lead singer of Generation X. Punk icon who left the shores of the Green and Pleasant to make a career for himself as a video-fuelled MTV punk icon, now Los Angeles-based expat and still touring like a thirty-year old.

The writer and singer of Rebel Yell – one of the biggest single hits of all time. White Wedding. Eyes Without A Face. Singles that made him for life. The avowedly Warholian-in-aspect platinum blonde spikes (which are still there, if not as lustrous as they once were). The chiselled, gavelled cheekbones created through hours of work in the gym and, at one time, industrial quantities of Class A drugs. And the sneer he borrowed from Elvis and subsequently made his own. The English accent would surely have given it away. Fran must have been in rehab a long time, but then – she's a kid, he knows. Twenty three, twenty four. Tops. Half his age, easy.

Jesus, she may as well have been on another planet. What would she be listening to now? Rap? Hip Hop? Even Marilyn Manson would seem old hat to her, he ruminates further, sipping his coffee and thinking of what to say. Didn't Kanye say the other week he was bigger than the Beatles or something and half his Twitter acolytes asked who Paul McCartney was? I mean, Paul faccin McCartney???

Half of him is faintly annoyed. That half of his personality fuelled by the natural ego of the rock star. The King Rocker. The Platinum Punk God. That half that powers the brand that is Billy Idol.

The other half is relieved because by not recognising him, he is free. It's almost as if she's given him permission to be himself. William, Will, Bill, the person he was sixty years ago in Essex. The person he returns to when he mounts his Harley and his Triumph. Behind the full faced mask. The humanity behind the Idol. He doesn't enlighten her because here the latter half wins, and he replies to her question with the most basic English cop-out of all.

Oh, this and that, Billy says. Bit of this. Bit of that. Another coffee?

No. Keeps me awake at night. Need to go to the rest room, she says, picking up her cell phone and smoothly, without fuss, gets out from behind the table and saunters to the back. Billy notices that she has a slight limp – only slight – but she's hot, all swing and sway as she ambles, staring into her phone, her jet black hair half way down the spine of her leather jacket, tight blue jeans acting like twin reluctant sentries to slim, muscled, gymnast legs.

Wow.

Another phrase from his youth comes to him. Cor, blimey, and he has no idea where it came from other than the recesses of his enthusiastic consciousness. She disappears into the ladies, but her afterimage is burned on his retina.

Billy is between relationships and having Francesca on his pillion reminds him that it's been a bit too between for his liking.

He wonders … no … quit it, William. She's … she's … and he laughs to himself, shakes his head inside and finishes off his bagel.

She's half your bloody age, mate. You're old enough to be her dad … even…

No…

Don't say it…

Old enough to be her g…

But what if…

Out on the bike again. Half an hour later. The early afternoon sun hovering there, Ra, Amon Ra, the omnipresent, impassive orb nestling in a cobalt sky. He noticed coming out of the diner that the brilliant sun was tinged around its circumference by an indigo haze, the faintest of halos. He thought it might be pollution, but it's too clear for that on Highway One. Too fresh, too many ordinances.

The Coastal Commission: They run the coast of California like some green Gestapo.

He remembers reading that Indigo is a debatable colour, even though Newton put it on his original spectrum, but, then, orange is even more debatable, which means that the sun above him is an entity of pure theory.

Francesca, too – stunning, slender, sleek; behind him, her presence on his Harley as omniscient as the sun above, and equally as theoretical.

Inside, he laughs.

Sixty years old. Looks forty. One of the biggest stars in the world. Living in two countries, with as much money as he can humanly spend, the numbers of twenty classy women he could date stored on his cell phone. Respect from his peers, a sell-out U.S. tour on its way and a pantheon of unequalled punk-pop hits to his name and there is a part of him, he ponders, slightly maniacally, that would swap it all to go back in time for one day with Francesca.

What's the French dictum? Halve your age and add seven. Thirty seven.

Just one day, matey.

They pass through Manchester and Billy grins as he always does. He remembers Manchester, the original one, with the rain and the darkness. They say that when the Pistols played Manchester in seventy six, everyone in the crowd raced from the hall afterwards and formed punk bands.

Manchester, CA is a bit different. Did punk happen here? Would Billy have ever been a punk had he been born here? He doubts it.

A while after, Francesca taps him on the shoulder. Billy changes down the gears, slows down. They pull into a lot.

Can we stop? There's a spot round the next bend. I'd like to show you something, she says.

Billy nods. What if, he thinks, but says nothing but a humble, sure.

They turn into another picnic site above a fenced white cliff top. They remove helmets and as gracefully as her movements in the diner, she dismounts – an inelegant word for what she just did: She almost levitated. Fran walks to the clifftop and stands there. It's warm, not oppressively, but enough. No breeze. That sun...

For a while she says nothing, just stares down below at the sea, the lapping waves, the encroaching tide colliding with multi-millennial rock. What Billy believes is a cormorant, stretches its wings and flies from its perch, a flash of green and blue and silver, a hoarse, almost panicked squawk echoing in tiny caves. He has no idea if cormorants nest in America. He waits for her, but still she says nothing, looking serious, as if possessed by critical thoughts. He stands next to her. Billy has never been the most patient person.

What are we looking at, then? He asks.

Those rocks down there? She points with a bronzed finger almost directly below.

Yeh.

They were nearly my last resting place. A year and a half ago. Could have died here, she says, as if she were discussing a manicure, a sports score from a team she cares nothing about.

Okay.

I was at my lowest, my real lowest. My then boyfriend had just punched me in the face in this very spot.

Sorry, Billy replies, but Fran continues as if he had made no acknowledgement.

Told him I didn't want sex. Way too stoned. Speedballs and Mary Jane, from what I remember, it was a while ago. Maybe acid. We'd been to a party up by Fort Bragg – on the beach, surfers, skaters, a kinda rave. This was, like, four in the morning. He was out of it, but I was completely out of it. OMG. He said he was horny and pulled into this spot. I said no. I wasn't horny a bit. Drugs were like a replacement for sex, you know? They were, like, an end in itself. You've been to Tempus. You'll know what I mean.

Billy understands that. For an addict, drugs are the apex, the essential. Everything else is negotiable. You'd trade your girlfriend for a single pipe of crack, and your addict girlfriend would sell both of you: Fran's then boyfriend was clearly not in the same addict ball park.

I didn't want him or it, she continues. Didn't want him to touch me. I remember thinking that I wanted to feel the touch of the wind on my face and that was all. That's it. Just the wind touching my face. So the asshole kicked my ass all round the passenger seat and then threw me out of the car. Drove off and left me here. Worse than the beating he gave me, he took all the good stuff and left me without cigarettes. And my cell phone was in the glove compartment.

That's not good, Billy says, instinctively wanting to hunt down and kill the bloke that did this, a paternal impulse, while simultaneously wondering why she is telling him the story. She continues.

My ancestors believed that the wind is made of the restless spirits of the dead and that there are two types – essentially a good and an evil wind. When I was on the beach earlier that night, I remember thinking that this was a night of the dancing spirits, so, here, thinking about that, I picked myself up off the floor and walked to the edge of the cliff. At this point, here, where we're standing, I could sense the ghosts of the past. The tender embrace of warriors and braves and medicine men and shamen and my mother and mother's mother and hers, too. Gently touching my cheeks. The hands of my forefathers. I stood here, and I cried. Then I climbed on top of this barrier, and stared into the void below.

She drifts off. Her eyes water.

Billy so wants to put his arm around her, but he stands, stock still. In that instant, he feels a gentle gust.

What happened? He asks.

Cops.

Cops?

Yep. Well, a cop. He pulled me off the railing, she says. I wasn't happy at the time, but now, I owe him my life. Turns out he saw me as he biked past. Highway Patrol. How, I don't know. It was late night, early morning. And it was dark. Maybe, those spirits weren't ready for me. The next day, I ended up in Bethlehem.

Been there, Billy says, agreeing, in sympathy. Been there, too.

And then, following some more epic adventures with lowlife dudes and totally unawesome mind-fucking merchandise, I found myself in Tempus. Clean and sober since and always will be. But this clifftop was the place that changed my life.

Pretty cool, Billy says.

I just wanted to share that with you. Do you mind?

Of course not, he replies.

And do you know something?

What?

That cop...

What about him, Billy replies. She is smiling, much wider than she has done so far. He has that warm chocolate and rising marshmallow feeling inside when she does so.

He looked like you. In fact, when you picked me up back there, I thought he had come back.

The cop that saved you?

Yeh, she replies. Except he didn't have an English accent.

Billy laughs. That would be just too weird.

Awesome, she says, joining in the joy.

The two of them stare at the mysteries of the sea for the longest time.

Later, early evening, on the road, a couple of hours to go before he plans to crash. Light rain begins to fall, coming from nowhere, the drops tapping on his helmet, a staccato drumbeat. He notices a subtle change in temperature. Within minutes, the skies above had turned jet-black. That kind of rapid fire Pacific madness, that insane volatility that belies the name.

At the end of the biggest drought in California's history, rainfall would be a cause for celebration, but for Billy and Fran, on a bike, it's shitty news.

Thunder strikes. For a split-second Billy feels himself lose control of the bike, just a tremor, just an impulse, like those inexplicable compulsions that beset every human from time-to-time; the ones that compel you to crash your motor into the toll booth, or to jump off the mountainside, or to take your pistol out of the holster, put it in your mouth and blow your brains out, those split-second sporadic itches that leave you unsettled and guilty for hours after, but he steadies himself as the rain falls in sheets onto the blacktop, saturating both of them instantly and making the bike skid, the handles difficult to grip.

Drenched, Billy spots an illumination up ahead. A motel, with diner. Like a firefly, he follows the light at thirty and he drives onto the gravel. Finds shelter under an awning. The two of them don't stand on ceremony –

they race for the diner as the black rain bounces and drums on the unyielding surface of the lot. Like shaggy dogs, the two of them shake themselves near-dry at the doorway to the diner; Fran making her way swiftly to the ladies room, while Billy commandeers the nearest booth.

The place is busy and, unlike in Britain, the locals eating their evening meals are staring through the window at the driving, pounding rain with something like joy. It had been months and the restrictions had bit everyone except the rich.

The waitress arrives with her pad. She recognises him straight away and beams broadly.

Are you...

Yeh, I am. Billy grins, with a sense of relief that makes him feel a little awkward.

OMG, I just love your music ... this is so exciting.

Cheers, Billy replies, grinning.

Their conversation is halted by a slamming door. A youthful-looking trucker in jeans and a soaking blue tee shirt arrives. He's wearing a cowboy hat, a black one, rather than the obligatory ball cap. One arm takes the form of an indecipherably tattooed sleeve. He is soaking wet, saturated in the short journey from his cab to the diner. The waitress is distracted, but only for that second. She returns to her request.

Would you sign my pad for me? She says, genuinely delighted.

Course I will, love, Billy replies, and he does so, with a swish and a swirl. Then, he orders food, and coffee, taking a guess at the former, and the waitress, her day brightened in wild contrast to the apocalyptic weather outside, returns to her domain, to be replaced in his vision by Fran, returning from the back.

What would I call this chapter, Billy thinks, reminded by the whole surreal situation of his recent smash hit biography. Not only does the waitress recognise him, but several other diners do, too. They are staring, but Fran doesn't notice.

The Girl Who Didn't Recognise Me. Has to be!

The waitress brings coffee, overjoyed.

Friendly waitress, Fran says, as disconnected and incorporeal as much of her conversation. She's like a bloody character in a modern novel, Billy realises, yet her cool, measured, comme ci, comme ça delivery is entirely at odds with her charisma, her aura, her absorbing presence. Only once has Fran displayed much more than a grin of resignation. Unlike the waitress, who is talking animatedly to the short order grill chef under the lamplight.

Yeh, totally, Billy replies, watching her sip her coffee and scrunch the last remaining moisture from her hair, tying it back into a ponytail.

He watches her eat eggs silently, noticing that she occasionally looks at her cell phone. They aren't going anywhere in that rain, he realises. He asks Fran to check the weather. She does. She tells him that this rain isn't going to pass any time soon. It's getting dusky outside, the outline impression of the sun, obscured by clouds, beginning to melt into the horizon.

What to do.

This is a pain in the ass, she says. I don't have any money aside ten bucks, and I've got nowhere to stay – I thought I'd be in Oregon tonight.

You might have been if it weren't for this rain, Billy replies.

Yep. A drought for months and then…

Pretty rare, Billy says.

There is a second of silence as the rain lashes the windows. Above the ocean, a flash of lightning illuminates the pregnant sky a dazzling, shocking blue. Fran leans forward on her elbows, and she gives Billy a look he knows of old, and well.

Listen, can you pay for a room? I'll wire you my share when I get to my friend's place. I have a job waiting for me, and I'll be able to pay back what I owe. I'll sleep on the couch … I mean … if that's okay…

It happens quickly. In a trice. For the first time, Fran looks unsure of herself, as if she had overstepped the mark with that last comment. Billy, who plans to get a motel room – I mean, what else can he do? – would gladly pay for the room. The money isn't an issue, and he'd never ask for it back, and he had already thought the motel proposition through before the first sip of hot, bitter coffee passed his lips.

I mean, she continues, if that's okay. If that's okay with you.

He mumbles an affirmation and as he does so, for an instant, time stands still.

He looks round. Strangely, there is silence. No clatter of cutlery on plates, no hubbub and low frequency chatter. The child crying at the back is mysteriously content. The everyday banter of the kitchen staff ceases.

Everyone in the diner focuses on the booth containing the sixty year old rock star and the tanned beauty young enough to be his daughter.

Even Fran has stopped still along with time. They all watch Billy. And like the mirrored Pacific he saw earlier in Bodega, reflecting the empty azure sky, he stares back at them, one by one.

The diners. The truckers. The waitress. The family of four from Humboldt County who have just arrived. Highway Patrolman Duke. The grill chef ceases his flipping and flopping. Leans on the immaculately clean counter. The blonde on the cash register stops mid-press.

They're all watching Billy.
It is a fragment in crystal.
What are you going to do, Billy?
Devil and Angel.
Devil and Angel on your shoulders.
What are you going to do, Billy?

Fran is a victim, he suspects. One of those women who men can't help but exploit. Something about her. Her cool, measured exterior a defence mechanism easily shattered. A front. He looks at her and knows she has an unfortunate chink in her armour for bad boys, drunks, druggies, gangbangers, dealers, losers, beaters, fighters, no-marks, bikers, musicians and low-life, a fatal Achilles Heel. He suspects that she is one of those girls that uses sex as an affection gathering tool (please like me, please like me, please, please) and subsequently, inevitably, paradoxically, she encounters men who have no intention of giving her a single comforting spoon after they've laid her down.

Billy, the King Rocker can see it, can understand it.

He's been there, done that, and he can see it in her eyes.

He's met a hundred – nay, a thousand – Frans.

And if the sex doesn't work in getting what you want, which is love, what you've got left is the drugs, and they hit the spot every time – no need for the arms of a good man around you when you've met Charlie and all his multi-coloured happy friends.

Billy Idol wants to fuck her. The King Rocker. Let's be honest. That's what Billy Idol does and that's what the audience encased in crystal glass wants him to do. Even if he paid for a separate room, which is the obvious thing, it wouldn't be long before she'd be in his, he can see it in her eyes now, and as she presumably doesn't drink, the small talk would inevitably – and quickly – turn into big sex.

BIG fucking sex.

And Billy, thirty years older, would treat her exactly the same way as all of them – the men she's escaped from, the losers who robbed her, the dealers who beat her and made her do shit things for drugs.

Billy would be the same. He's the King Rocker.

He's the King of Punk, the lone survivor, fighting off all comers.

The King of the Pride.

They've all gone. The Pistols. The Stranglers. The Clash. All of them.

You're the last man standing, Billy.

Why shouldn't you enjoy the fruits of your reign?

Why?

And he looks at her over the table.

He knows he can have her.

And he wants her, wants her, wants her, wants her.

Billy Idol wants Fran.

Hearts engraved with a box cutter on chipboard desks.

Fran 4 Eva

SWALK.
Now.
In the motel.
Do it.

But that's Billy Idol. A man she doesn't recognise. A man from another world. An alien presence.

It's William she knows, this lovely afternoon on Highway One.

William.

Freedom. And that changes everything.

Fran's cell phone goes off and she signals that she's going to the ladies. Billy watches her movements and knows he is going to regret this next move. The only move he can make. The crystallised audience melts and carries on with its dinery business.

He gets up, moves over to meet a new face, sits down. Shakes hands. Negotiates…

Ten minutes later, she returns to the table, and she looks fresh and clean and young and gorgeous. The trucker is sitting next to Billy, and he offers his hand to a startled Fran.

This is Tex, Fran.

Hi, she says, confused.

I've just had a quick natter with him, Billy says. He's on the way to Oregon and has to get there in the morning. He's on his way now.

But… Fran says, knowing what is coming next.

He knows exactly where you're going, and he's offered to give you a ride up there.

Fran says nothing. Tex acknowledges her warmly and says he has to go tidy his cab, and he shakes hands with Billy, leaving the two of them together.

I thought, she says. We could...

Billy leans toward her, puts his hand on her cheek and pushes a curtain of hair back over her shoulder. Then he reaches into his jacket pocket and hands her a sheaf of greenbacks and a napkin on which he has written down his cell phone number.

This is to get you started up there, he says. With your friends. And when you get the time, when you've settled in, when you're feeling comfortable about the place and your creative juices are flowing, yeh, I want you to paint me a landscape. On canvas. You said you paint, right?

Sure do, she says, a tear forming on the corner of a reddened eye. I told you.

That was no bullshit? You paint, yeh?

No bullshit, she says, crying. I paint.

When you've painted the painting for me, something magnificent, something I can look at forever, I want you to text me sometime in the summer, when it's done, when it's the best landscape you can paint, and I'll bike up here, and I'll take your painting and place it above the mantelpiece back at my house, yeh? And it will remind me of the terrific afternoon we've spent together. How does that sound?

She mops up her tears, a vulnerable, fundamentally shy girl, bombed back to the stone-age by the world, but now on the way back.

Okay, she says.

And no dick paintings. I couldn't put those up in my living room, now could I?

She laughs, lightly.

No dick paintings, I promise. Tex... she queries.

He's a good kid. Don't worry. I've sorted him out proper – he'll make sure you'll be totally safe, I assure you. You'll be with your pals in three hours, no problem.

Fran sits back. Secures the cash and card in the zipped upper pocket on her leather jacket. Considers saying something, but thinks better of it. Then, she smiles broadly.

It will be the best painting ever, William. The absolute best. I mean it. It will be an awesome painting.

I wouldn't expect anything else, Billy says.

Thank you, William. For all this. Thank you.

No worries, Fran. And you're welcome.

He stands and so does she. The two embrace, a warm, endless cuddle and for a millisecond, feeling her next to him, Billy feels the devilish impulse to cancel the whole deal, all of it, and take her back to his room, but he fights it, smells her unique essence one last time and kisses her on the cheek. She cries as he walks her to the door.

Tex has pulled up outside, and she jumps up into his cab.

Drives off into the rainy night.

Billy watches the truck depart. He imagines Fran waving out of the window briefly and then, the giant Mack turns right onto the rain-swept highway, spray from the deepening puddles on either side as high and lofty as surf. He waves back to nothing and inside, he grins.

Back in his booth, other diners come, the news of his presence spreading like wildfire, and he goes to work, happily signing autographs and taking compliments about his music and – most heartening – his most recent tour, the one he did at sixty. He tells them all to come and see him in L.A. and in Frisco and if they can't make that, then he tells them about Vegas in March and in May. He sips coffee and then, picking up his helmet, he waves everyone goodbye, giving Verna a kiss on the cheek and allowing her to take a mobile phone selfie with him.

That is Billy she's in love with.

The King Rocker with the sneer and the spikes and the attitude.

The English envoy to the court of American rock and roll.

That's Billy, but as he strolls to the motel next to the diner, taking a long hard look at the falling rain descending from platinum, almost molten grey skies, splashing in shards an inch high up his black leather boots, he realises that Fran had no clue about Billy and all that time, she was talking to William and that's all she will ever know, well met, and well met.

He leans back on the wooden wall of the bike shelter. Watches the rain fall and feels the wind on his face, the external environment he experiences inside. Next year, after the tour, Billy plans to motorcycle to some great landmarks. The Transfaragaran Highway in Romania and the corkscrew of the Stelvio in Northern Italy. If his management will let him. All the insurance people. All the apparatchiks.

Fuck it, he says to himself I'm just going to do it anyway.

He loves his bike. And he loves the freedom.

And maybe a little part of him loved Fran, too.

No, a big part.

He pats the silver and blue petrol tank of his Harley. Wonders whether he will meet anyone like Fran again.

At sixty, he hopes so.

Jim Kavanagh
© Brenda Perlin | BlossomingPress.com

Punk in New York City
1977-1981
Jim Kavanagh
© 2016

Jim Kavanagh owns a small Construction firm in New York City. When he is not working for Fortune 500 companies, he spends time with his sons. He is a stout conservationist who is dedicated to saving the Big Cats. Forever a punk, Jim ran in the streets of NYC from 1977-1981 and lived the "no future" political movement of the times.

Punk in New York City was a lifestyle, not the weekend fad it fast became in the video era. Like the hippies that proceeded us, and the beatniks before them, Manhattan Island seemed like the only allowable playground for our group. Although a number of us lived in the outer boroughs, it was just a short subway ride into the City.

New York City was our home. We could be found in Greenwich, East or West Village, occupying benches from Tomkins Square Park on the Lower East Side (at St Mark's Place) to the West Side Piers. Most days, I was skateboarding in Washington Square Park (West 4th and Macdougal entrance), doing what someone who looked like me often did – selling drugs. Heck, it was better and more profitable than odds-and-ends construction labor! Not too many business owners were hip about hiring us because of the way we looked.

New York University, the prestigious College located around Washington Square Park had plenty of students and sales were good. Since our stash was hidden nearby, very little was on our person. We also had a lookout team that managed to keep us safe from the occasional sting. We supplied celebrities who enjoyed the anonymity and the buzz off our product, which was anything you could imagine. Sadly, we often used a portion of our profits for our own recreational enjoyment.

I stood a little over six feet tall and weighed one hundred and eighty-five pounds in those days, and wore my natural color blonde hair in a tall fin with a tight crew cut on the sides. Faded and torn blue jeans were tucked into untied army jump boots, accessorized with a black studded leather belt that matched my wristlets, dungarees jacket, or vest (leather came later), a torn T-shirt with some hand-drawn mockery on it, tattoos and a boom box.

Of course, makeup and the fin only went up when we frequented the bars and clubs at night. I often simulated car tire tracks across my face with dark eye shadow, and I spent at least an hour, and a ton of gelatin, to get my hair just right as the effects of two Quaaludes kicked in. During the day, those of us with complicated hair would wear berets or bandannas, but I quickly adapted to a short spike look after summer, just because it was easier.

The cops always fucked with us, but after multiple frisks they found nothing; messing our hair ticked us off, which set the tone for a bad night. All that work destroyed by some *ass hat* wearing leather gloves who was pissed because we bested him that evening.

Never fuck with the hair unless you want to brawl was our motto. To this day, just reminiscing about it makes me angry.

I used to fear family functions that I had to attend, having to borrow "normal" clothes and shoes that never fit, although, I did always appreciate clean socks. Never ever could I say "no" to my mother. A saint, if there ever was one.

Taming and slicking back a seven-inch fin that took me months to perfect, was usually an ordeal to have it look semi-"normal." But the style was a focus of conversation with my parents' friends during whatever event it was that I attended. Oddly, I liked the attention my tattoos would get.

Listening to the Pistols and the anarchy it started in Britain was something we all related to. Here in America, we were looking at interest rates at nineteen percent, inflation off the charts, double-digit unemployment and hostages in Iran were held for over a year. So yeah, we found our outlet: Punk Fucking Rock!!!!

There were only a few crossover rock bands we heard at the clubs: Stones, Zepp, AC/DC and Ozzy. We hated the Who and Quadrophenia and that Mod crap. It was gross that people called us Mods in later years, which pissed us off.

Then again, everything pissed us off.

Christoph Fischer self portrait
© Brenda Perlin | BlossomingPress.com

Rebel Yell
Christoph Fischer
© 2016

Christoph Fischer was born in Germany, but currently lives in West Wales with his partner and two Labradoodles. Christoph writes 20th Century Historical Fiction, contemporary family dramas and crime fiction.

The year was 1984. I was a slightly overweight teenager and looked young for my age – which at the time was the opposite of what I wanted to be. I was a reluctant altar boy, trapped in a life, which wasn't me, and I had no clue how to get out. I should have been content, only, I felt like I didn't belong in this world. I had neither the means nor the know-how to find an answer to my questions. I was a wannabe rebel without a proper cause.

One thing I did know was that I envied my tall and sporty school mates, many of whom hid behind the sports hall and smoked cigarettes after class. They were the tough guys who didn't conform to the unwritten rules of our Bavarian, rural small town.

One of these guys was particularly charismatic: Alex. Our parents knew each other, and I got to spend many afternoons with him and his brother due to parental arrangements. My cheesy music tastes, however, were not for him, and he must have suffered a lot in those days – a lot as a result of being forced to entertain me. Kim Wilde and the more commercial albums by Van Halen were as much musical middle ground as we could establish.

Alex was mainly into Iron Maiden, and thanks to his open-minded mother, he wore leather metal jackets, leather wrists bands and used hair products. I so wanted to be like him.

My mother was less liberal as far as my clothing was concerned, and my pocket money didn't stretch far, either. My attempts to copy his style were admittedly more entertaining than provoking.

Amateurish experiments to shape my hair with sugary water failed miserably and the local hairdresser, a close friend of my mother's, would not grab his scissors without conferring with her first. I was damned to look normal.

During one of those days we spent together at his house, Alex introduced me to Billy Idol and his music, and my heart beat faster (and my gay teenage hormones were romping mad, too).

Alex could stick his tongue out exactly as Billy did in the videos that shocked and provoked our parents when we watched the chart shows together. I tried to copy him in the mirror, but to no avail. Although I couldn't quite work out how I would go about it, I knew that this was much closer to who and what I wanted to be than the altar boy persona, which my Catholic family had in mind for me.

Alex's style went to more extremes as Punk made its mark on the Zeitgeist and one day, our Latin teacher had enough and made him sit in the last row so she wouldn't have to look at him and his 'offensive outfits' close up. Her intended insult shocked the more timid ones of us but it 'Idol'-ised Alex in our eyes and made him the hero of our class. Another girl came to school the next day with an involved punk hair-cut in blue and purple. She was also sent to the back of the room. God, I was jealous of them and wished I had the backbone to go against my family and do the same. It would be a few more years before I started sneaking out of the house at night, smoking, drinking and emancipating myself from the norm.

In 1984, I struggled. Encouraged by others at last, I bravely broke into my piggy bank and bought a metal leather belt and matching wrist band to wear at school. I may have looked like a tit, but I felt like a real rebel.

My hair was far too stubborn for an imitation mowheecan cut, but I had at least managed against all nagging to grow a long toll that would dangle into my face, and that week I took a bus to the next town and dyed it blue. This abruptly ended my days as an altar boy.

At that stage, however, the novelty had worn off as quite a few of our students had followed the new trend and sported new wave and punk accessories. Imitator that I may have been, I felt liberated all the same. Perhaps, I was too soft to become a real punk; the rebel spirit of the times, however, laid important foundations that came to fruition later in my life. Billy and his mates have, in their way, still shaped and contributed a lot to my life with their provocative and daring attitudes.

That winter, our class went to a ski camp in Austria. Every evening, we used the communal hall as a place of worship to our idol music, and we played the songs of our (musical) idols. "This is not a love song" by P.I.L. was our declared favourite. Over thirty years have passed, but the punk rock spirit and the rebel lyrics still yell "more, more, more."

Jorge P. Newbery
© Brenda Perlin | BlossomingPress.com

Burn Zones
Excerpt
Jorge P. Newbery
© 2015 – 2016

Jorge P. Newbery founded Upstart Records, which released seven collections from bands such as Stalag 13, Circle One and Red Scare. He crafted Youth Manifesto, a cassette magazine featuring Black Flag, Bad Religion among others, and also promoted gigs throughout Southern California.

"Go ahead, throw one more bottle, you punks," the officers appeared to think as they eyed the kids outside SIR that night. "Just give me an excuse to beat you dozens of times with this club. Let me work out some of this pent-up frustration." This was well before handheld video cameras and Rodney King, so as soon as a punk threw one projectile too many, the LAPD army had the justification they yearned for to indiscriminately dispense adrenaline-fueled drubbings on fans. This escalated into a full riot that shut down Sunset and several adjoining streets. Some fans split to avoid the pandemonium, while others were itching to rumble and joined the cops in escalating the situation. Although the raw tension was electric, I stayed calm.

I had been through this before at other shows and learned to walk away and avoid the chaos. I was appalled at the behavior of the police, but also by some of the punks. "Two wrongs don't make a right" is a well-worn cliché, but it was apt here. Setting fire to police cars to get back at the cops for beating your friend may have made a fan feel good for a moment, but in the end, this resulted in venues like SIR and the Whisky banning punk shows. We all lost.

Caddy Rowland attending Halloween party
dressed as Ziggy Stardust
© Brenda Perlin | BlossomingPress.com

Punk Paradise, Minnesota Style
Caddy Rowland
© 2016

Caddy Rowland makes a living writing gritty, raw, graphic fiction for adults. Her genres include psychological thrillers, drama, and historical fiction. She also writes gay m/m romance under the pen name Sibley Jackson.

Back in the seventies, there weren't many bands in the USA showcasing punk. CBGB's was the heartbeat of punk in this country, but there were a few others, which sprang up, giving those of us thirsting for something more than what we were being force-fed on the airwaves a hearty slug of in your face punk, new wave, and alternative rock.

Jay's Longhorn Bar in Minneapolis was one of the premier nightclubs to offer us salvation from the disco scene, which had invaded the Twin Cities with a passion. Ah, God, what a relief it was the first time my husband, Dave, and I walked downstairs and into The Longhorn! We'd been listening to Bowie, Lou Reed, Iggy, and the New York Dolls albums, praying for the day we could actually hear some decent music live. Until the punk / new wave scene hit, the seventies music scene sucked (although as a Minnesota girl, I did have a weakness for Prince).

We weren't into hanging with the bands, although there were a few we followed from venue to venue just to hear them play. Nor did we get chummy with many. We weren't looking for friends, we were looking for escape. And we found it in the music and the dancing. God, the music. I'd get lost in the music as soon as we entered the dark cavern of the dance area, forgetting all the work bullshit; the life worries. All that mattered was the music and to move. Once we started hangin' at the 'Horn, one could pretty much find us there five nights a week. We might have struggled to pay rent, but we always had money for the Longhorn. It helped that they had reasonable drink prices.

Plus, once the bartender got to know us, he made sure to pour a more than generous amount of booze in our drinks. I personally had a weakness for Bacardi 151 Rum and Coke, with a bottle of beer for a chase. Yeah, I could have two of those drinks and still function decently. Therefore, I'd sip on a beer in between drink number one and two—and for the rest of the night, I'd order beer with an occasional water.

At the time, we both smoked. I remember wondering if my drink would catch fire when I flicked my lighter because it was poured so stiff. My drink and our beers would be waiting for us by the time we walked across the floor. Once my drink looked more clear than brown and, as I mentioned earlier, I drank rum Bacardi 151 with Coke. I had to tell the bartender I appreciated his generosity, but unless he wanted me dead, I needed a couple more glasses half filled with cola.

And, let me tell you, that bartender was special. He looked exactly like Elvis Costello. In fact, I'd have sworn it was Costello behind the bar. He was also totally into the sound. I don't know how he did it, but that man could pick up your money from the bar, spin around with one leg high in the air, open the till by smacking it with his fist, put your money in, grab your change, slam it shut, and slide your change back in front of you in one revolution. It never took him more than the one spin. It helped that drinks and beers were even dollar amounts, I'm sure, but it still seems an impossible feat to me, even to this day.

We never talked to him much because the music was so loud one had to shout to be heard. And that was the point, right? The music ruled everything. But that bartender came close. I never think of the Longhorn without thinking of him. Oddly enough, his name escapes me although his face doesn't. Then again, this all took place over thirty-five years ago. Sue me, my mind just isn't as clear as it used to be.

There were many regulars at the Longhorn. One was a chick named Karen, who had Ziggy Stardust hair and elbow length fingerless gloves. I think they were either red or orange. Every time we were there, we saw a guy who always came alone and danced alone, right smack in front of the huge amplifier closest to the bar. He was in his own world, doing Chuck Berry-like guitar moves back and forth in front of a small part of the dance floor. As far as I know, he never talked to anyone.

Speaking of the dance floor, it had to be one of the biggest in the Twin Cities. In fact, the whole place was huge. One entered by going down some stairs. There was also a room upstairs, but I don't think we ever ventured in, or if we did, I faintly remember a few pool tables, and you couldn't hear the music as well. Again, my mind is hazy about it, so I can't be sure.

When you got downstairs, there was a cocktail lounge one could enter to the left. Another area we seldom frequented, but we did go in once and sat at a wooden booth when we brought another couple with us. We wanted them to discover punk. I believe it was the last time we saw them. Ah, well. The music mattered more, anyway.

Straight ahead brought you into a huge, somewhat dingy room with a long bar over to the left if you were facing the stage, which was almost as soon as you got in, and there were also a few wobbly cocktail tables and chairs.

And then, there was the dance floor. It was more the size of an old ballroom. I never saw the whole dance floor taken up. That was great, we could get as wild as we pleased. Since I was taking prescription speed, I was always up for dancing as much as possible. I couldn't eat, but I sure could dance, smoke, and drink.

You can bet, if the music was playing, you'd find me out there on the floor, usually in tight shiny black pants. I topped them with an old neon orange mini-skirt worn as a shirt, over one shoulder with the other shoulder bare. I tightened it around my waist with a thick gold metallic belt that looked like snake scales. It clasped with a huge, funky buckle. The belt had been my mom's way back in the 1930's or 40's.

Other times, I wore authentic parachute pants bought cheap at the Army Surplus store, which hung far below my navel. They were paired with a black and white striped tube top and a black beret perched far back on my head. It was pinned down so it wouldn't fly off when I danced, standing proudly, like a halo, up behind my head.

I also favored skintight black peg leg jeans or the green Army fatigue pants, which hung even lower on my hips than the parachute pants, with a washed out blue T-shirt featuring the face of Brian Eno with the words "Eno is God" below it. And, of course, I always wore lots of black eyeliner. Sometimes, I even made my lips black, and was clever about using black eye shadow to emphasize my then stellar cheekbones.

Although many chicks wore heels, I didn't. I was tall, and I was flying. With our total abandonment to the music, I'd have fallen on my ass in heels. Instead, I usually wore black ballet slipper-type shoes.

Why I was given this prescription for speed remains a mystery. Regardless, at the time I thought the doctor was great. I was already thin as hell, he continued to refill it for months. But, hey, it made me think I could do anything, until paranoia started setting in. But that is another story still a way off in the future.

Females at the Longhorn had to have a deep love for punk music and balls made of concrete. This was because the women's bathroom was straight from hell. Every single night we were there, all of the women's toilets overflowed. We hung at the 'Horn for about four years and never once did those toilets fail to spew water and piss all over the bathroom floor. You had no choice but to walk through piss to piss! Unless, of course, you enjoyed peeing your pants. I was never a fan of wet pants, so I braved the piss-covered floor. More than one pair of ballet slippers saw their demise after a night at the Longhorn.

I've talked to several old punkers from England who said every punk bar was the same. It seems one thing we all had in common was piss-filled bathrooms, and not giving a shit because the music was too good to stay away. One old punker remarked, "God, what a punk song that would've been: Piss Walkin' Punks." I think he was on to something.

The Replacements, a Minneapolis band, and Husker Du, a St. Paul band, both cut their teeth at the Longhorn. The Replacements are still playing today, after a break-up for a couple years. The Replacements lost their hard edge punk years ago, back in the 80s, morphing into something else, though still great. It's funny how, even now, many think of them as hard core punk. If those people had been around to hear their first stuff, they'd know how they sounded when they were really punk. I don't think I've ever heard a louder band.

Husker Du went from hardcore punk to alternative rock before breaking up in 1988. It wasn't a friendly break-up and for years it stayed that way. Recently, they launched a website, selling Husker Du T-shirts. It remains to be seen if there will be a real reunion. The three are communicating again, which is positive. When I think of the times I saw Husker Du, the thing that sticks out in my mind is how fast they played. What a blast to dance to!

Some of the other regular local bands at the Longhorn were the Suburbs, Soul Asylum (alternative rock), the Flamin' Ohs (our personal favorite), Curtiss A, the Dad's, the Wallets, and the Hypstrz. But the band who was first in regard to punk in Minneapolis was the Suicide Commandos. They began in 1975, before the Longhorn even existed. The Suicide Commandos released two albums. The first was titled Make a Record, and the second was The Suicide Commandos Commit Suicide Dance Concert, which was a live album done in 1979. It was their last performance together. However, their last performance at the Longhorn had been in November of 1978.

The Longhorn had a steady stream of bands performing from New York, England, and other places. The Clash, Buzzcocks, Blondie, Gang of Four, Talking Heads, Dead Boys, Robert Gordon, Mink De Ville, Iggy Pop, The Stranglers, The Police, Naked Raygun, The Effigies, Pere Ubu, The Plasmatics, Elvis Costello, The Nerves, Peter Hammill, Willie Nile, and The Squeeze to mention some. Not all of these were punk, obviously. Some were new wave, some were alternative.

I wish I could say I saw them all, but I didn't. It's funny how when you're in the moment and feel like you're in Utopia, you think it's gonna last forever. We were young, things came up, and we assumed the bands would keep coming back. The Longhorn was my reality, my place to go where being alive became a high-charged, energy pulsing, no holds barred thing. I was whenever Dave and I stepped into the Longhorn. The rest of the time I simply existed.

Now? Now I realize those few years were the most precious, the best of my life. And, as the cliché says: All good things must come to an end.

R.I.P. Jay's Longhorn Bar. You'll be remembered always. The memories will be accompanied with a bittersweet smile, while the deepest part of me keens to relive the past. Like the best of lovers, you took away a piece of my heart. And the majority of my soul.

Alison Braun self portrait
© Brenda Perlin | BlossomingPress.com

In Memory of a Pistol Packing Reganite
Alison Braun
© 2016

Originally from Los Angeles, Alison Braun photographed punk bands and wrote for several music fanzines under the name MOUSE from 1980-1990. She currently resides in Seattle, Washington.

It seems for most movements involving youth and popular culture, there was a certain credo around hating our parents or hating any figures of authority held up in our daily lives. It was as much a part of our punk uniforms as combat boots and homemade tee-shirts.

There have been innumerable song lyrics and ramblings in various zines about recounting those horrible battles we have with those beings responsible for bringing us into our despairing existence.

It's a little funny when I look back on that period of my life through the lens of an official "old person", entering the half century mark.

I fell into the punk subculture in 1980, mostly because of the influence of older friends, but also because the anger and in-your-face-energy really spoke to me and filled a need for independence from the usual dramas of adolescence. The irony of the whole thing was that I took my father (the resident authority figure and keeper of the word "NO") along for the ride and turned him into an unwitting participant in the L.A. punk movement. Without this dreaded parental figure tagging along with me, I would have never realized my potential as a photographer and writer documenting the underground scene.

It started as a challenge. I wanted to go into South Central Los Angeles for a show. My mother confronted me with a tactic she was certain any teenager would recoil from: "There is no way you are going there without your father." My response was immediate and direct. "Okay, let's go."

Why is this even a story? It's not really that interesting. But it is.

My father was a Regan supporter and did a short stint in the FBI. He was also anti-gay, and mostly intolerant of any racial makeup other than his own – White and Jewish. He grew up in Brooklyn; never went to college, and like most of his contemporaries, went off to war (WWII). He was a genuine anachronism to people my age. He grew up without a microwave for God's sake! Live music in his book meant Benny Goodman at Carnegie Hall.

The most punk thing a person could do was to change people's mind from within. When done correctly, it was so effective, they didn't even realize you were a catalyst and instigator.

And therein started a side bar in the annals of the L.A. scene, Alison (AKA, MOUSE) the photographer and her thoroughly uncool dad with his lexicon of totally embarrassing post WWII slang, packing a legally concealed 38, and chauffeuring me from show to show, or dutifully waiting outside for me to emerge for a ride home. Sometimes, he would venture in and slide up to the bar, sharing drinks with a milieu of Hollywood characters.

My father ended up holding court at the Cathay de Grande sipping beers with El Duce (Mentors), loaning a tie to Biafra (Dead Kennedys), for his court dates, and hosted a steady trail of drag queens, Goths and rock stars over to our house. His mind opened in ways I never knew possible.

Dad broke up a fight at Godzilla's, not because two idiots were fighting, but because he thought it wasn't a fair fight. He confronted the cops at a downtown riot and excoriated them for the use of excessive force. People at clubs started to remember his name and, eventually, stopped recoiling when they frisked him and found that dang gun of his holstered inside his jacket.

He enabled a trust in me that should have been reserved for someone far beyond my years. At any time, my father could have put a stop to my punk rock activities and shipped me off to some girl's school in Provo, Utah, but he didn't. I kept my grades up, purposely steered clear of drugs, and was completely open and honest about where I was going and what I was doing.

It was because of this partnership with my father that I was able to document the punk ideology and amass a huge archive of photos. Without him, my path may have been much different and less colorful.

I dedicate my punkdom to Stanley Braun who was willing to open his mind and support his bratty kid while she found her creative muse in a setting that usually hated parents.

Steven E. Metz
photograph © Glen E. Friedman / My Rules

Listen to a Fifth Grader
Steven E. Metz
© 2016

Steven Metz teaches at Earth's Power Yoga in Los Angeles and is the inventor of Yogascape, a completely immersive surround video environment.

The Hideaway in Downtown Los Angeles

A club promoter known for promoting very famous shows during the 70s decided to take a shot at the L.A. Punk scene. So what does he do? He books Black Flag, Castration Squad, Circle Jerks, Geza X, and our band, Mad Society. I was only ten at the time, by the way, and the rest of the band wasn't much older.

In 1980, even just Black Flag would pack the place by itself, but mixing these bands into one show was like trying to put a skyscraper into a shoe box. Also, they served no alcohol, allowed no ins and outs and hired a group of long-haired New Wave dancers to perform in a frame apparatus on stage as a backdrop behind us. They were dancing like Fred Astaire, not slamming, like punks did in the early 1980s.

I am sure you can see where this is going.

During a sound check at about 3:00 pm, I had enough of the fashion crimes I had seen and spoke with the promoter.

Steven: You know that punks don't dance like that, and the outfits they are wearing is not a good idea.

Promoter: I am trying to create something different. They will love them; they just don't know it yet.

Steven: I am telling you they are going to throw stuff at them. You don't know this crowd like I do.

Promoter: I will take care of it; don't worry about it. I have been doing this for years, and I know what I am doing.

There is an old saying, and I think it is Germanic. Gegazun to heit. Basically, it means, move aside, may "the way" be with you, please step aside, there is someone behind you that will heed my advice.

Castration Squad went on with no issues and no dancers. I was really happy. Punks were slamming, and the show was going well.

We went on the stage and while we are playing our tune, Napalm, the dancers came out. They were dressed in spandex with cutout sections and see-through plastic pieces showing their skin in various sections; they used temporary hair color and teased it up. Basically, he hired a bunch of "posers", and it was a direct insult. If you used temporary dye, you were a poser; that's it, either cut your hair and be with us or don't and get beat up. They had long hair, too; a very big mistake. Punks and hippies mix as well as fire and gunpowder.

Our L.A. punks responded by throwing bottles and records. They were flying over my head and hitting the dancers behind me. Needless to say, the dancers ran off the stage.

We played about two more songs and next thing I knew, the wall at the front of the room got kicked down and lit on fire.

The combination of no alcohol and no ins and outs caused a lot of anger at the entrance. They ended up ramming the promoter's gold Rolls Royce through the front door to get back into the club. The Riot Squad showed up, and we had to roll our equipment out. We barely escaped with our gear, and a bunch of our friends got hurt.

I learned a lot that night. Do your research. Know the environment your clientele likes. Heed advice from those with more experience in the particular field you are attempting to participate in.

Moral of the story? Sometimes, you have to listen to a fifth grader.

The Damned
© Brenda Perlin | BlossomingPress.com

Godzilla's
Brenda Perlin
© 2016

Brenda Perlin originates from California and has never left the state. Her books are based upon personal experiences. Brenda is passionate about music and supporting animal rescue programs.

Peering through the huge metal door, I could see my friends' restless faces. I patted down my hair and wiped my lips dry with the back of my wrist as I prepared my usual speech.

"Just wait, you guys. Shhhh. Don't tell anyone. I'll get you in when no one's around. Chill out and try not to be obvious."

That was me working the makeshift hamburger stand at Godzilla's night club. The music was wafting through the club's speakers. The Sex Pistols, God Save The Queen, flooded my senses while my boyfriend tried flipping burgers like it was a pizza joint. All I could do was roll my eyes and act like I was busy. I didn't put too much into this job, obviously – for me, it was a way to see cool bands for free. Free was the magic word since I didn't have a job. I mean, a real job, one I took seriously. I was too busy being a punk and everything that went along with that.

Punk was not a fad to us. It had a violent image that was not always deserved. They said we were out of control. A bad reputation followed us around, and we were considered angry youth. Maybe, we were more than that. I mean, we were teenagers and outcasts. Who is not a little bit angry when you are being told what to do all the time?

We simply wanted to have a good time – and boy, did we ever! Late nights playing around with friends. Laughing and goofing off without parental supervision. Creative with our hairstyles and clothes. Talking non-stop about the bands we were going to see next.

This was not the rebellion that people thought it was. No. Maybe, this was the case in the U.K., where the kids couldn't get jobs and had good reason to be pissed off, but for us, we owned the land, and the music thundered through our veins.

Godzilla's in Sun Valley, in the northeast corner of the San Fernando Valley, was a new punk club that opened on December 4, 1981. It became our base. Frank Reed owned the place, a man who got his start booking punk bands at Devonshire Downs. When he located this building, he hired Sean and Mark Stern to coordinate booking and security. For a while, there had been no problems with the police or punks, thanks to a peer security force called the 'Better Youth Organization' (B.Y.O.) – teen punks from Huntington Beach, Oxnard, Hollywood and the Valley.

The club was a former bowling alley, consisting of five large rooms, which could be filled with fifteen hundred people at a time. There was a grungy feel with the coffee shop, "Godzilla's Grill", and the massive music area – all concrete floors, surrounded by chain-link fencing. Spray-painted along one wall was "Punks don't fight. Save the club." Another, we completely covered with our own graffiti.

Working there meant I could spend time with my friends, meet bands and get paid. Godzilla's was another stab at giving punk a chance somewhere other than Hollywood where there were big riots going down and clubs were being closed left and right.

My friends and I flocked to Godzilla's even when I wasn't working there. We congregated around the grimy streets, often begging passers-by to buy booze for us as we were underage. More often than not, we were successful and drank more than our share of cheap liquor. We roamed the surrounding neighborhood as if we had taken up residence. We must have looked frightening with our spiked-up hair, Mohawks, black make-up and bondage pants mixed with a vintage flair. Most of us were not violent at all. We were just misfits trying to fit in and have a good time.

My boyfriend, Patrick, and I managed to stay together while we worked the Grill. The job wasn't that hard, and we felt like punk rock royalty because we thought we had a little bit of clout. And we did – we got to watch the musicians do their sound checks and that was a big deal.

The two of us met The Damned, which might have been the most exciting thing that ever happened to me. These guys played right in front of us, and we could talk to them while they were setting-up. They were real guys with big personalities, who were not too different than we were. I might have been star-struck, but I tried not to let it show. I played it cool, as if it was just another day, but I didn't always succeed. When they rehearsed New Rose, I got goose bumps that made the hair stand up on the back of my neck. It was like I had been plugged into a light socket. While the room seemed to be spinning around and around, all eyes were glued to the stage.

At Godzilla's, there was always a good band to see, even if they were not well known. This was our chance to discover new talent, and we could smell it a mile away. On stage, we witnessed futures come to life. Our friends from Woodland Hills, Bad Religion, made their start at Godzilla's. At the time, they were an unknown, unsigned band and just a few short years later, they went on to hit the charts.

We met so many of our favorite local bands. After all, they were one of us. The Circle Jerks, Social Distortion and T.S.O.L. were important bands, and we followed them everywhere they played.

The slam dancing was beyond belief, even though I was only a spectator. Watching the guys jump about was a riot. I loved the buzz and the heavy booming of the music, the vibrancy of the people, the way they looked in their wild outfits; an amazing sight. Mesmerizing. I never bored of such an environment. The stimulation was such that I didn't know where to look next, who to talk to first. Waves of energy pumped through the atmosphere, and I had never been so alive.

Idiots getting violent damaged the vibe on occasion, but most of the time it was just kids having fun and enjoying being in the moment. When good bands played, the room was on fire. It was electric. Nothing else mattered but what was going on in the here and now.

It's a wonder Godzilla's was able to stay in business as long as it did – though, really, looking back thirty years or so, it probably wasn't open all that long. A punk nightclub in Sun Valley might not have been the best idea, but whatever – us teen punks took advantage of it as long as we could.

The plan worked out well for a while until the Fire Department got wind of what was going on, paid us a visit and uncovered some serious wiring problems. The whole place was a firetrap! Not only that, but they discovered the club didn't have an occupancy permit. That was the beginning of the end, but at the time we didn't know it.

Godzilla's was run by punks for punks. It was not only about the music. It became something holy. Once closed, we were lost. It was as if someone had shut down our cathedral. This club gave us a place to worship – not only the punk music, but the culture. Here, we were a part of events that mattered, and it was sacred.

Janet Salopek Green self portrait
© Brenda Perlin | BlossomingPress.com

What Punk Rock Gave Me
Janet Salopek Green
© 2016

Janet Salopek Green was born in Santa Barbara, but grew up in the suburbs of Los Angeles. She survived punk rock and a bad marriage while raising three awesome kids. Still residing in Los Angeles, Janet is employed by a technology company.

My narrative is dedicated to all the people that have not only impacted my life then, but still do today. Sadly, some have passed. This story is for all of us.

I was a Catholic School Girl.
I went to Catholic School my whole life, including an all-girl High School.

In first grade, I got into trouble for arguing that if God is Love then there is no Hell.

I grew up in the San Fernando Valley, but I didn't want to be just another "Valley Girl."

I knew from early on that I did not fit the mold.

Music is often the center of any young adult life. Rodney on the Rock, Phases, Country Club, Starwood, Madame Wongs, Bards Apollo, Brave Dog, Vex, Devonshire Downs. If you were there, these names stir memories as unique as the time.

It was a new era, or at least one in a series of generational eras. We were post Peace and Love, being too cynical and not trusting tomorrow would come. We doubted we would live to see twenty five much less fifty. Many did not, and now we have begun a new procession of passings – a combination of old age and hard lives. Recently, they announced David Bowie's death. Anyone born in the sixties or seventies would feel the impact of that genius of a man, but I digress.

Music was like a virus that invaded my life, ever changing and constantly reflecting my view of the world, or my mood, or my attempt to moderate my emotions.

You might laugh, but for me, it started with artists and groups like David Bowie, B52's, X, the Ventures, and like a drug, I couldn't get enough. The great angst of teens combined with a growing lack of faith in the adults that were running the world needed an outlet.

We chose clothes often influenced by the bands we loved. Our clothing was an outward expression of how we wanted to be seen. For me, this meant frequenting a treasure trove of thrift stores in the Valley during the late seventies, early eighties. I fell in love with old school feminine clothes from the forties to the sixties, but always added a twist, such as wearing a pencil skirt with a bustier, but removing the blouse once outside the house. I often wore a Catholic school uniform skirt donned with a denim jacket with Harley wings and cowboy boots, at other times, wearing Dickies and white tees.

I met Cindy and the Stains at a party in the Hollywood Hills. Louie was a flirt and Cindy thought it was ridiculous that I was wearing a tulle skirt/dress. Somehow, I got thrown in the pool, and we've been fast friends ever since. Humor – there was lots of funny shit that happened like that.

Keep in mind this was the age before cell phones and the Internet. Not everyone had cars and getting to a gig was a challenge, especially since we were out several nights a week and every weekend.

We had all the trappings and traditions of teenagers from every generation – crushes and loves – scandal and drama – hickies and the Hickie Hotel – and of course, drugs and alcohol, although the narcotics took too many away from us too soon.

After the gigs, we often hung out at Okie Dogs, chatting, socializing and planning the next event while eating, puking and trying not to be arrested during frequent altercations.

Being a Catholic school girl, the running joke about me was "to the altar or to the grave." I was that weird virgin. My father had told me I would be better off committing suicide than coming home pregnant. I was more afraid of him than social pressure so I waited until my second year in college. Upon graduating from High School, my rather stoic parents insisted I throw a graduation party. At the time, I was dating Mike Muir from Suicidal Tendencies, and the band decided they would provide the music. As one could imagine, the party just got bigger and bigger. For some unknown reason, my parents also had invited their best friends, and my dad was the bartender. Think about that for a moment. Catastrophe just waiting to happen. However, that night, he laughed and actually got along with everyone.

During the party, Jay Adams (famous Dogtown skater) was doing something crazy. (I know shocking right?) I have a picture of my 5'2" mom threatening him with her cane. Oddly, things were fine for a while. There was an odd mix of people from my high school (ninety-five percent were not into punk) mixing with skaters, surfers, and every possible flavor of punk, until it happened...

Someone was leaving to attend an event in Hollywood as I recall. When they were walking to their car, the jocks from the neighborhood were returning from some CIF playoffs, and a huge fight ensued. The punks ran through the neighbor's house breaking windows. No one was seriously hurt, at least not there, although the friendship between my parents and that family was severed. I also left home and never lived with my parents again. I would visit, but it was not the same. Later that same night, Jay got into a terrible fight in Hollywood, but that is not my story to tell.

More often than not, fights did not result in serious injury. But there were many exceptions. People died. Got arrested. Served time. Lives were changed. Paths redirected.

It was not all bad, nor all good. Someone's mother once pointed out that while we all thought we were so original, we had simply changed uniforms. If we truly accepted individuality, we would not have needed to fight over being different (or something to that effect).

There were many deaths, each more painful than the last. At some point, it became too depressing for me. The joy of the wanton excitement was gone. Drugs and alcohol have that effect, taking away the glow. I drifted off into the reggae scene, which was perpendicular and concurrent (another long story).

There are many people from those days who remain in touch, and I am grateful for these contacts. We have chosen a variety of paths, but so much history together cannot be forgotten, and we do have a lot in common.

For that reason, I thank Brenda Perlin for the opportunity to add one of my memories to the list. I may have figured out that anarchy didn't work for me, but I am still trying to find that place to call home.

I am not ashamed to say I love so many of these people whether or not I have spoken to them recently. It was like living through a war, of sorts, together, and we are still here.

A special shout out to Becca, who is earning a Ph.D. degree. Who would have thought? (Congratulations, Becca) I'm proud to call this motley crew family.

Punk Rock gave a disparate set of outcasts a community. Something to care about or not. Somewhere to shine. Somewhere to fit in. A voice. The means to survive or die trying.

Jim Kavanagh self portrait
© Brenda Perlin | BlossomingPress.com

December 1980
Jim Kavanagh
© 2016

Jim Kavanagh owns a small Construction firm in New York City. When he is not working for Fortune 500 companies, he spends time with his sons. He is a stout conservationist who is dedicated to saving the Big Cats. Forever a punk, Jim ran in the streets of NYC from 1977-1981 and lived the "no future" political movement of the times.

The year was 1980 and the Punks were on their way to establishing a strong following in NYC

It was a strange year all around. Ronald Reagan was on the march to become President of the United States. Iran would not free American Hostages. We would fail miserably in April with an operation to save those hostages: The results? Eight dead servicemen.

America's political sense and our economy were splitting at the seam.

In December, the day after the 39th anniversary of the attack on Pearl Harbor, on a chilly winter evening in NYC, John Lennon was shot and killed.

I remember sitting on a bench in the "park" listening to the Buzzcocks, and friends arguing about the effects the grain embargo was really having on Russia. We always sounded off by sharing our opinions of everyday politics, sports and media crap. Not surprisingly, most people from a distance would listen and laugh about the subject of our conversations.

We were always animated and quick to educate those that never realized Punk was more than music. Of course, over the years all these so-called "experts" will tell you plenty about Punk and its roots but don't be fooled: at that time in the late 70's and early 80's, we were considered misfits and not to be taken seriously.

Anyway...

Nobody in our group of Mohawks, spikes and leathers knew what to say or how to handle Lennon's death. From my recollection, Darby's death was glazed over and barely mentioned.

Darby Crash killed himself on December 7th, Pearl Harbor Day 1980. Lennon's murder the next evening occupied everything in the media. All media!

At the time, I struggled trying to put this into a perspective I could deal with. As a kid, I loved the Beatles and John was my favorite Beatle. Most found it to be a taboo subject. In our Punk atmosphere, to acknowledge the impact of the death of John Lennon would have been confusing for us. Nobody wanted to see this as a part of our definition of punk.

But, John's death magnified the continued social collapse of that time's culture. Nothing was sacred, and we were not happy. NO FUTURE was again our motto. John's death was now a great format for us to continue the Anarchy.

Sid had been dead twenty-two months, and we were so tired of telling those who saw us in all our regalia, where the fucking Hotel Chelsea was. (Where Sid killed himself.) Whoever thought that would become such a tourist location! I hear it's a five-year wait to stay in the same hotel room...

Now, the "new" question from the tourists was "Where is the Dakota building?" (Where Lennon was gunned down.)

NYC planned a Vigil. Ten minutes of silence for John Lennon.

Middle of the day ... NYC ... Quiet!!

Well, we had other plans and decided as a group that we were going to crash this vigil and send a message to everyone. Our message? Another hot topic that was never defined. I was so high I could only listen to this idiotic debate. Although I did eventually agree to go uptown with everyone and become part of this "show" that we planned put on.

So ... fighting the urge to nod, I found the energy to somehow, get my hair just right, lace the boots and put on my white "Disco Sucks" T-shirt.

Quick Note: From 1970 to 1971, Rock and Roll lost Jimi Hendrix, Janis Joplin and Jim Morrison. In 1980, we lost Bon Scott, John Bonham and of course, John Lennon.

I remember the scene we made in the subway ride uptown as we got closer to 72nd Street. The train quickly became packed with people crying. Young and old. Strangers just weeping openly to one another. The adrenalin that surged through me straightened me up in seconds. I remember looking at my friends stunned. Here we were, the definition of NYC Punk looking at this train full of people with the exact stares we had received for years. We were completely dumfounded.

As we slowly worked our way off the train and up to the street, 72nd and Central Park West was a mob scene. We could barely move. The entire area was wall-to-wall people of every denomination and culture. The sidewalks, the streets. You just couldn't move. Every radio station shut down to honor the silence.

When the vigil began, none of us said a word.

You just couldn't.

It was a very quiet train ride back to the park for us. We didn't do any of the things we planned, but we all walked away touched in some way.

Our innocence was officially gone.

In that moment, we became veterans of a scene that years later, people still try to define. In my humble opinion, nobody has got it right yet.

And to the point of Punk, you're not supposed define it, or worse, categorize us.

Like Art, Punk is subjective. The NYC Punk genre was different to everyone who lived it. Lennon's death and those 10 minutes of silence galvanized a time for me. Nothing was the same after that and nothing would ever be the same again.

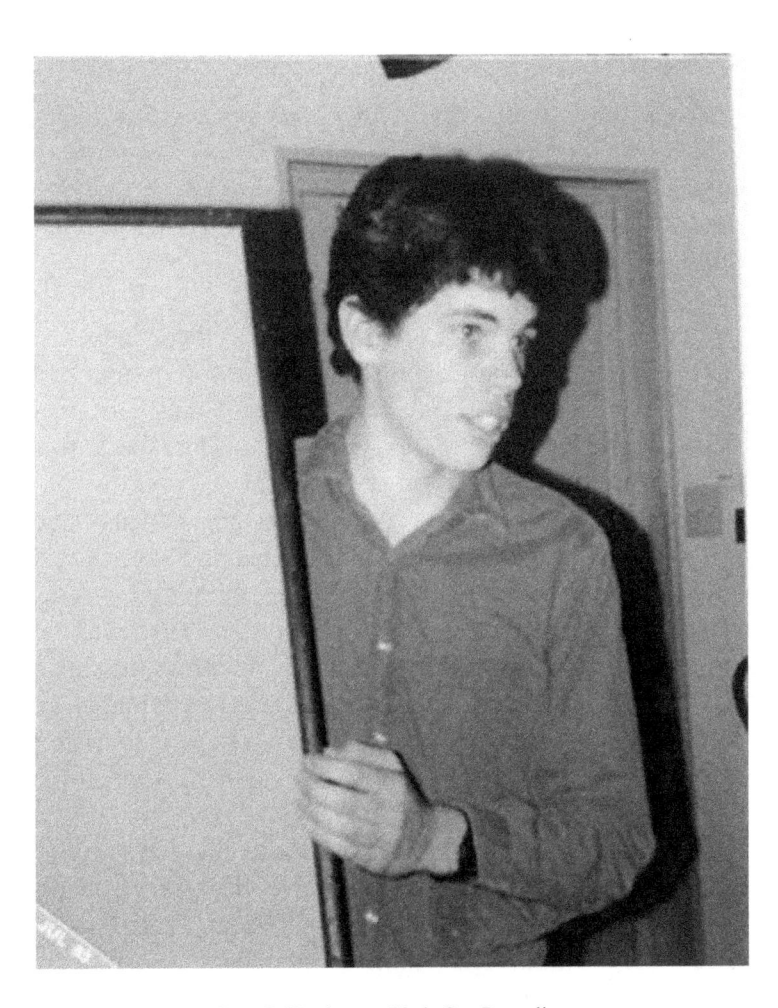

Jorge P. Newbery at Circle One Recording
© Brenda Perlin | BlossomingPress.com

Burn Zones
Excerpt
Jorge P. Newbery
© 2015 – 2016

Jorge P. Newbery founded Upstart Records, which released seven collections from bands such as Stalag 13, Circle One and Red Scare. He crafted Youth Manifesto, a cassette magazine featuring Black Flag, Bad Religion among others, and also promoted gigs throughout Southern California.

I convinced my father to drop me off at the Whisky-A-Go-Go in Hollywood on Sunset Boulevard to go alone to the 8:00 PM all ages Saturday shows. I saw Britain's Killing Joke, local bands 45 Grave, Monitor, the Circle Jerks, Wasted Youth and others.

The youthful energy of the performers and the audience was contagious, and I slammed and stage dived with abandon. At school dances, I always felt awkward as I publicly displayed my lack of rhythm. However, at punk shows, I could freely join in the swirl of the mosh pit. No rhythm needed. I felt this was where I belonged.

"Do you need a ride?" I would be asked over and over from a parade of smiling men in nice cars as I stood at the bus stop across Sunset from the Whisky.

"No, thank you," I replied. "My dad is on his way to pick me up." I didn't understand why the locals in West Hollywood were so helpful. They all seem so friendly, I remember thinking. I didn't understand just how "friendly" they were trying to be until a couple years later.

Christoph Fischer and friend
© Brenda Perlin | BlossomingPress.com

A Night To Remember
Christoph Fischer
© 2016

Christoph Fischer was born in Germany, but currently lives in West Wales with his partner and two Labradoodles. Christoph writes 20th Century Historical Fiction, contemporary family dramas and crime fiction.

My student days became my rebel years. As soon as I could, I moved away from what I perceived as stagnant and conservative Bavaria and relocated to the opposite end of Germany; I grew long hair and listened to Cyndi Lauper, "The Cure", "The Ramones", "The Clash" and "The Damned." I was ready to take on the world, and was always willing to protest for good causes. There wasn't a month when I didn't join a sit-in or one protest march or another. I worked for the Student Union and enjoyed arguing with the authorities.

I longed to be free and without overbearing laws and restrictions. I felt there were too many rules and regulations. There was overwhelming agreement about that feeling amongst my friends, in our class rooms and on the alternative dance floors I frequented.

I dyed my hair black, orange and blond, wore leather and jeans and gained confidence through my dealings with the campus administration. I had since come out as gay and the long suffering altar boy inside of me wanted to take to the streets about it, and was biding his time for a good opportunity to do so. It came via a group of punks.

The punks I met at the university canteen were political. On weekends, amongst other activities, they held regular gay kiss-ins and protest rallies outside country churches to demand marriage equality (although the word wasn't yet used). I wasn't a proper punk, but I sympathized with their cause and occasionally joined them.

Some were part of a group squatting in an abandoned theatre house in the centre of Hamburg. The derelict building was used for underground concerts and illegal housing, surprisingly tolerated by the 'Democratic' city administration and frequently and generously overlooked when redevelopment plans were being drawn. As the commune was running out of money to keep going, they organised a series of fund raising events. A provocative gay clubbing event was planned, 'For the Lady in you' with an added auction of souvenirs from their weekend adventures to educate the bourgeoisie.

None of us believed in the conventional institution of marriage; we pointed out injustice, provoked the smug and voiced our distaste for the establishment. While these events were pretty harmless within Hamburg, very liberal and open in character, outside the city limits these activities were a bit of a dare. The requests to get gay marriages from the priests usually resulted in fist fights with the local church goers. I attended one such kiss-in that needed police intervention. The result was an auction item in the shape of a piece of uniform, ripped out by one of the police dogs that day.

Proud to have been part of the action, I couldn't wait for the final fundraising event. To get the much needed student discount for said clubbing night, one had to come 'dressed as a real lady' to the event. I had never done drag, but was still fired up from the shouting match with the church goers during the weekend before. I borrowed a mini skirt, leather boots and make-up to gain my reduced entry. Since I lived a long way out of town and had no way of getting home at the end of the night, a friend kindly lent me his taxi for the evening.

There were live bands, head banging, dancing pogo style, a feeling of raging against the machine and the deluded impression of overwhelming invincibility. Sadly, the city had just announced redevelopment plans for the theatre area the week before. We knew our case was now lost, but we had a hell of a time at the wake for our project. Exhausted at 5am, sober but over-excited still, I packed the car full of my drunken friends and began the long drive across the city of Hamburg to drop them home. My mates were still fired up and chanted political slogans and sang along loudly to "Why Can't I Be You", "How Beautiful You Are", and "Kiss Me, Kiss Me, Kiss

Me" off of my new Cure tape, Disintegration. We didn't get far before the police stopped our clunker. When the officers approached the car, the two stopped shouting but also fell into a giggling fit. I got out immediately to demonstrate my sober state and to placate the situation. Unfortunately, even though I had switched the motor off and taken the key out of the ignition, the engine was still running. I was so confused that I completely forgot about my attire. The police officers were equally perplexed by both the car and me. The three of us stood stunned in silence, looking back and forth between each other and the running car.

Meanwhile, the laughing increased. The officers caught themselves and checked my driver's license, the vehicle papers and used a breathalyzer on me. Once it was established that I wasn't drunk, they remained unsure about what to do about my taxi. I persuaded them to call the owner at home. This was before mobile phones, and they had to go through a complicated process via their base.

The laughter continued, gradually infecting me, albeit certainly not the officers. When my friend told me in a sleepy voice over the phone that I had to lift the bonnet and find the 'Stop' button, I thought he was pulling my leg. I repeated these instructions, trying to keep a straight face until the giggles got to me, too, and I doubled over on the pavement.

One of the officers snapped and put us in the back of his police vehicle to be taken into custody. As worried as we were about the consequences, the laughter wouldn't stop. Another police patrol arrived on the scene. To my amazement, he opened the bonnet of the taxi and found the legendary 'Stop' button. Who would have thought?

The patrol teams conferred for a while and to my relief, we were free to go. A week later, I received a letter with an informal warning about proper conduct with the authorities. A trophy I hung on the wall by my desk at the student union. It was a night to remember.

Iggy Pop 1977
By Michael Markos
Picture Credit: Wikimedia Commons

The Riot House
A Fictional Tale
Erin McGowan
© 2016

Erin McGowan is a writer, accountant, publisher, and baker. Author of Aftermath, and The Mage: Awakening, her short stories have been published in several anthology collections. Erin enjoys listening to music while roaming around Galveston Island off the Gulf Coast of Texas.

When I look back on the first night I spent at the Riot House, what comes to mind is a quote from the movie, Clerks. You know the one: that guy, telling everyone that he wasn't even supposed to be there on that day. Well, I wasn't supposed to be at the Riot House. I was supposed to be in bed. In fact, that's where I was until I heard a noise outside my window.

All I wanted was a good night's sleep before a big Algebra test the next day, but something had definitely hit the ground hard outside my window, and Mary's room was right above mine. Mary, my older sister, was the wild child in the family. She thought our nice, normal life in a nice, normal neighborhood just outside of Los Angeles was boring, predictable, and stale. The rest of us didn't much care one way or the other. I didn't want my mother's life working part-time in a clothing store and raising four kids, but I didn't want to go out and raise hell with Mary, either. I wanted to go to college to have a career in ... something. To do that, I needed good grades, which meant I needed to get that good night's sleep and do well on my Algebra test.

But curiosity got the better of me.

I pushed my frilly, white curtain aside to get a good look at our yard and saw my sister get up from the ground and brush herself off. Cursing and calling her every name I could think of, I threw on the first skirt and blouse I could find. I was scared that this would be the night my sister might follow so many punk footsteps and shoot heroin into her veins. I couldn't take that chance. Time was not my friend, so I found some comfortable flats and brushed my long, brown hair into a tail. Under any other circumstances, I'd never leave the house looking so unkempt, but I consoled myself by pointing out that the only people I was likely to see were Mary's friends. From what I could tell, those kids and their heroes didn't even own mirrors. They never matched and thought that safety pins were acceptable accessories. And then there was the music.

I couldn't stand the music my sister and her friends listened to. They called it rock n' roll, but I knew better. The Eagles were a rock band. Iggy Pop made noise and hurt himself. I'd tried to understand it. I'd listened to what they liked to call music. I had no choice; the walls in our house were paper-thin. I couldn't wrap my head around it any more than I could wrap my head around their lifestyle. These punks took drugs, got into fights, ran away from home, and at least one of them made my life infinitely harder in her quest to have a good time.

Yet, I was the idiot dashing out the back door of the house, cutting through yards, and sliding into the taxi right behind my stupid sister at ten on a Thursday night.

"What the hell, Kimber?" Mary shrieked as I shut the door of the cab. "He was about to take off. You could have gotten hurt."

"It's Kimberly," I sniffed. "My name is Kimberly. And clearly, you don't care about anyone getting hurt, least of all Mom and Dad. Where are you going?"

"Look around, lil' sis," Mary said with a chuckle. "We are going, unless you want to jump out. Bowie is supposed to be at the Riot House tonight. Rumor has it he sprung Iggy, and there's a wicked party to celebrate his freedom. I'm not hurting anyone, anyway. I'm just trying to live my life. You should try it sometime."

"I was," I grumbled. "You are aware that none of these people actually care about you, right? None of them know who you are. They just use you for gratification."

"They all know me," she argued. "Maybe they don't know sweet little Mary, but they know Starlight, and they love her. They come to me for inspiration, friendship, and sex. I go to them for the same things. You wouldn't understand. You're so busy trying to get ahead and make the grade that you've forgotten how to live. How to be a friend. You forgot how to have fun. Well tonight, you're going to remember. Tonight you are Kimber, and we're going to have an amazing time at this party."

"You can do whatever you want," I said, slouching against the dirty seat. "I'm going to pay this nice man to take me right back home as soon as we get to … where is this place again?"

"The Sunset Strip, baby," Mary all but howled. "And if you leave, I'm going to try smack tonight. You have to stay to keep me clean."

Damn her. My sister knew my worst fear was that she'd try drugs. I figured she probably already had, but I was also pretty sure that she'd kept to the shallow end of the pool. Even I had tried marijuana. I didn't want her to end up like her idol, Janis Joplin, and she was using it to force my hand.

"Fine, I'll stay," I said. "I don't have much of a choice, but you can forget this Kimber business. Tonight is not going to haunt me for the rest of my life. Come up with something that doesn't tie into my name."

"Yes, sir," Mary said, saluting me.

"What about Twisted?" the cab driver asked, surprising us both. "She's all twisted up, ya know?"

This sent Mary into a fit of giggles.

"That's perfect," she said, still laughing. "Tonight you're Twisted. And now the show begins."

Sure enough, the taxi pulled up to the curb and stopped. Mary paid the driver, then prodded me to open the door and get out. I was greeted by a wall of sound and a milling pool of humanity. Every freak in the world was on the Sunset Strip. Unfortunately, so was I.

I reached for my purse to make sure I had money for a cab home and realized that I hadn't brought my purse, my ID, or any money with me. Laughing, Mary propelled me through the crowd and into a building that was just as busy as the sidewalk that fed it. The lobby of the hotel, if you could call it that, didn't do much to alleviate my fears about the night ahead. It didn't just resemble a motel lobby, it resembled a seedy motel lobby. Some nut rode his loud motorcycle by us as Mary steered me toward the elevator bank. Groupies and fans and other members of the unwashed masses whispered and giggled with each other in groups for an insanely short amount of time before they broke apart and formed new groups. Peeling and stained wallpaper and paint covered the walls, and I heard a crack as the motorcycle passed us, indicating that another poor, pitiful tile had given up the ghost and joined its multiple broken brethren.

I heaved a sigh of relief once the elevator doors swished shut, which was a mistake. We stood at the front of the elevator with at least half a dozen other people behind us, and from the rank quality of the air I stupidly inhaled, none of them believed in bathing, and at least one of them loved rancid perfume. I didn't dare look behind me for fear of who or what I would see. In the last ten minutes, I'd glimpsed enough safety pins through skin, Mohawks, and made-up men and women to last a lifetime. I was not especially religious but decided that the best way to get through the rest of the night would be to close my eyes and pray.

That's exactly what I was doing when I heard the doors slide open and the ding that indicated we were there – wherever there was. Mary linked her arm through mine, and I opened my eyes, against my better judgment, so I wouldn't run myself into a wall – or worse, a freak.

My sister pushed and shoved our way down the hall to one of the many crowded rooms with their doors propped open. My sister let go of me just in time to keep both of us from being knocked down by a little sprite of a girl who wore way too much makeup and tight leather pants.

The sprite threw her arms around Mary and squealed, "Starlight! Now the party really has started."

"Mystic, darling, I should have known you'd be here," Mary said, hugging the girl back. "I'd love you to meet my sister, Twisted. Twisted, this is the sweetest girl in the world, Mystic."

"Cool name," Mystic said, walking around me like she was sizing me up for a date … or a fight. "Doesn't really match your look, though. Did you think you were going to the library tonight? Maybe, you'd pop in on the local Republican's tea?"

"Fundraiser," I snipped. "They might meet for a speech, but political parties are generally too busy to have tea for the sake of having tea. That's not how these things work."

"She's my sister," Mary said with a shrug, addressing Mystic and the rest of the freaks who were looking at me like I had two heads. "She jumped in my cab. What could I do?"

"Nothing, angel," a guy with stringy blond hair and no body fat said as he put his arm around my sister. He didn't have a shirt on, and I could count his ribs. I could also see scars all over his body, and I got the feeling that the man was not exactly sober. "We all understand how annoying straight relations can be, Starlight."

I crossed my arms and huffed my way all the way out to the balcony, ignoring everyone. I didn't need their approval and didn't care what they thought.

Another too-skinny man was sitting on the balcony with an acoustic guitar in his lap. This one wore a suit and a serious expression, but his mane of reddish hair and guitar gave him away.

"Hello there," he said, with an English accent. "Where's the fire?"

"I don't think there is one ... yet," I replied. "But there's enough smoke in there that I'm glad my flight led me out here."

"The question remains," he murmured, "what are you fleeing from?"

"My sister and your fellow noise fanatics," I sneered. "I'm supposed to be in bed. I have a really important test tomorrow, and it's almost eleven."

"So go home," he said. There was no heat or accusation in his voice. He was just stating the obvious.

"I can't," I confessed, lulled into trusting him by his mild manner and lack of animosity. I sat across from him and leaned my head back, letting the clean air and city noises sooth me. "My sister threatened to use hard drugs if I left. If it's in my power to stop her from going down that road, I will do it."

"Who is your sister?" he asked. "For that matter, who are you?"

"My sister is Starlight," I said, fighting a smile. The name was so ridiculous. "And for tonight, I am Twisted. Who are you?"

"David," he said. He stopped playing long enough to shake my hand. "I know Starlight. She's a good girl. I can't believe that she'd be stupid enough to go that far down the rabbit hole. Just in case, though."

He got to his feet, swaggered into the room, said a few words to a very beautiful woman, and came back out to join me on the floor of the balcony.

"My girl will take care of her," he said, flashing a stunning smile at me. "You can go if you want, but I would love to know more about you, Twisted."

"There isn't much to know," I said. "I'm the youngest of four. I want a career more than I want a family. I like rock music, but not your brand, and I value hard work. I want to walk the straight and narrow path."

"Have you listened to 'our brand' of music?" David asked as he picked out a rhythm on his guitar. "Have you ever tried to walk something other than the beaten path? What exactly do you want to do when you get done with school?"

"I have been forced to listen to my sister's and brother's idea of music. We share a record player and even when they take the thing to their rooms, I can still hear the noise," I grumbled. "The rest is none of your business. Especially since I doubt you could even find the beaten path, and you certainly don't know what hard work looks like."

"You think so?" he asked, chuckling. "I write songs, tour, promote, record new material, produce other people's albums, act, dance, and study. My life is full, to the point that I don't get to see my little boy very much at all, and I'm writing and recording on the road. Make no mistake, it is hard work, and it wears me down to nothing some days."

I was shocked by his admission. I tried to imagine the life he was describing and found that I couldn't do it. I had a hard enough time keeping up with schoolwork, chores, and extra-curricular activities.

"Why do you do it, then?" I asked.

"Love," he replied. "I love music. It's in me. It's a part of me. I look for people who love it as much as I do. I look for the geniuses who can create great music. I look for showstoppers and game changers. I know you think we're all freaks, and you are somehow convinced that being a freak is bad. Well, you're only half wrong. Yes, I am a freak, and I love it. I love things that are different. I love things that make me think, that challenge me. I love anything that pushes me out of my comfort zone. I love the strange. It pushes me to be more, better. Everything I see and hear and do drives me to be the best me I can be."

"Not this 'best me I can be' shit again," the blond, skinny guy with no shirt groaned as he joined us. "Sweetheart, keep in mind he's full of crap. The great and powerful Oz. The man who created and killed Ziggy Stardust. But we all know the truth. Ziggy wouldn't exist without me. He'd be nothing without the kids from the Factory, Angie, and me. Nothing." He yelled it out to the sky and spread his hands out like he was welcoming God. After that announcement, he turned and stalked back into the room without a word.

I looked at David and saw him shake his head, sadness filling his eyes. In that moment he wasn't a freak. He wasn't a stranger. He was a brother watching a man he loved dive straight into the deep end without a care in the world. I knew that feeling too well. I felt that exact way every time Mary left the house.

"He doesn't mean it," David rushed to assure me, or himself. "They shouldn't have taken him out of rehab, but I couldn't stop his so-called friends from helping him escape. I'll take him back tomorrow. It just kills me to see him like this. He's a genius, you know. A musical genius. No one can perform like him, and when he's sober you will never meet a sweeter guy."

"I'm familiar with the type," I murmured, looking into the hotel room, searching for Mary. She was on some guy's lap, laughing, with a bottle of whiskey in her hand.

"So, you never did answer my question," David said, drawing me back into the conversation and away from the door. "What do you want to be when you grow up, Twisted?"

"Honestly?" I asked, forcing myself to walk to the edge of the balcony and sitting down. David pulled out a cigarette and offered me the pack. I took one, feeling reckless. Why not be a little bad? I wasn't Kimberly tonight, after all. I was Twisted. So I lit up, and answered his question. "I have no idea. I want a career. That much I know. I don't want to be stuck at home, a slave to my husband and kids."

"Well, it's a start," David said. "What do you like to do? What subjects do you like in school? What do you do for fun?"

"I love English class," I said. "I enjoy reading and writing. I'm on the Yearbook Committee at school and sometimes, I pretend I'm a newspaperwoman and write articles, just for fun."

"Really? You're a writer, huh?" he asked, looking thoughtful and stroking his chin. "I know a guy you might want to talk to." David got up, wandered into the room, and came out a few minutes later with a piece of paper in his hand and a beautiful blonde woman trailing behind him. "Twisted, it is my pleasure to introduce my wife, Angie. Angie, this is Starlight's sister, Twisted."

"Twisted, huh?" the woman said, taking my hand and giving it a firm shake. That startled me, because I'd been taught to do the opposite. I rather liked how it felt, though. "You look more straight-laced than twisted to me."

"It was a little joke of my sister's," I admitted. "I didn't want her to use my real name, so she gave me a 'punk' name. Tonight, I feel pretty twisted up, though."

"If you're worried about your sister, don't be," Angie said, putting a hand on my shoulder. "She acts tough and loose, but she's a good girl in her heart. Plus, we're looking out for her, and I laid down the law with these guys. No one messes with me, especially when it comes to the girls."

She just looked so sweet and so capable that I felt compelled to believe her. I took what felt like my first real breath all night, then promptly started choking on cigarette smoke. That made all of us laugh. I took the time to cough it all out of my system before trying to speak.

"So, I can go home and she'll be alright?" I asked. "It's not that I am having a bad time. I'm having much more fun than I expected to, but I have a test tomorrow. I need to go home."

"I'll make you a deal," David said. "You can go home worry-free tonight. Tomorrow, though, I want you to come to my show. I'm playing a small gig at the Whisky with a few other bands. I want you to experience our music, live. I also want to introduce you to my friend, Lester."

"Please come," Angie seconded. "I would consider it a personal favor."

"But," I looked down, focusing on the toe I tried to work into the concrete.

"But what, love?" Angie asked.

"I like him," I said, looking her in the eye. "I like you. God help me, I even feel bad for the skinny, cut-up, drugged-out guy who's hitting on my sister. What if I still don't like your music?"

"Is that all?" David asked with a grin. "If you don't like it, you don't like it. It's not the end of the world. At least you gave it a shot. Come on, love. What do you say?"

I agreed to go to the concert and gave Angie my full name so she could put me on some list. They insisted on introducing me to everyone in the room, and even drew me into a few conversations. Oddly enough, the punks my sister hung out with became people as I got to know them. I didn't like all of them, but they became ... human.

I left a few hours later, much later than I'd planned. David and Angie insisted on walking me out. On the sidewalk, they gave me hugs and found me a cab. David even insisted on paying the taxi driver. I fell asleep as soon as my head hit the pillow, but woke up a few hours later when the back door opened. I knew that it was

Mary. I let out a breath of pure relief. Angie had kept her word. All I had to do was keep mine.

The next day, I slept through most of my classes. I also found myself looking at people differently. I listened to them, what they said, how they stated it. I started looking past the trappings, trying to see the people. It unnerved me. My test was not nearly as hard as I thought it would be. I left Algebra knowing that I passed with flying colors.

That night, Mary came to my room and asked if I was really going to David's concert.

"I am, actually," I said with a smile. "Can I borrow some clothes?"

"Of course, you can!" she crowed, grabbing my hand and pulling me up to her room. "I'm so happy you're coming. I thought you'd flake for sure."

"I like David and Angie," I admitted. "A few other people as well. I don't know about this Lester guy or writing for a living. Is that even done? But, maybe, you were right. Maybe, I should get out and experience more."

"Sure, people write for a living," Mary said with a laugh. "You read books, the newspaper and magazines. You think they don't pay the people who write those things? Just so you know, Lester is ... different. He's way more intense than David or even Iggy. Be careful."

"Always," I said, smiling at the thought of my carefree sister warning me to be careful. "No drugs tonight, right?"

"Absolutely none," she promised.

We left a little while later, dressed in getups I would have cringed over twenty-four hours earlier. I couldn't say what came over me. I just wanted to be different. I wanted to try something new. Perhaps, I wanted to see why the punk life appealed to my sister and people like her friend, David.

We got in without any problems, and they even escorted us backstage. I knew a lot of the people, but there were many more that Mary knew and I didn't. We spent the hour before the show socializing. I found a group of people who were talking about things that actually interested me and stayed put. Mary flitted from group to group like a butterfly on speed. I watched her warily. I couldn't help it. Her blond, too-skinny friend was there, and he stuck close to my sister. That made me very nervous.

Soon things started happening. Musicians were getting organized to go on. The rest of us were shuffled out of the way. David grabbed me and made sure I went with Angie to a good spot just off of the stage.

"David, why is your friend here?" I asked, throwing another worried glance at the blond and my sister. "I thought he was going back to rehabilitation today."

"He talked my darling husband into letting him play tonight," Angie interjected. "We're taking him back tomorrow."

"He promised to stay sober if we'd let him play tonight," David said. I nodded, still uneasy.

There were so many bands that they each played only a few songs. There were some I liked, some I loved. David was one of the musicians I fell in love with that night. I saw a dark-haired man with a mustache staring at me quite a bit, but he seemed more curious than interested. I wondered about him, but never asked Angie or my sister. I wanted to stay focused on the music, even the stuff I didn't get.

Mary's blond friend, Iggy, as it turned out, went onstage and blew my world apart. He was totally different out there. He was beautiful, amazing. He made me feel the music and the lyrics. He showed me a new world. When he left the stage, I screamed my enjoyment along with the crowd and the other people on the side of the stage. We all fell for him that night. Some of them had fallen before and would fall again. He was just that magical.

Others were not. There were plenty of bands that made me want to run for earplugs. Others knew how to play and sing, but couldn't draw me in. It was like they didn't connect to their music.

This amazing band that took us all to a different place closed the show. The announcer called them "The Who." I just knew that they had it – that magical quality that David and Iggy had, that thing that made you want to follow them to the ends of the earth. It was the perfect way to close the night. Little did I know the night was just beginning.

David and Iggy made a line straight for us, and David dragged me over to the man who had stared at me all night. He was Lester Bangs, and he was just as intense as Mary had said. I spent most of the night getting grilled by him about my thoughts on the show and the people who had played. By the time he stopped asking me questions, I wanted to run away from him. He offered to answer any questions I had, but I couldn't think of anything to ask.

"You wore the poor girl out, Lester," Angie said. "I wouldn't want to work for you if I was her."

"How else am I supposed to find out anything?" he countered.

"Read her writing, silly man," Iggy said as he passed us.

"There's no need," Lester said. "She's got the right temperament, eye and ear, but she doesn't need to be a rock critic."

"I don't want to be a rock critic," I said. "And I'm right here. Talk to me, not about me."

"Fine," he grumbled. "I can hook you up with some people at the paper here. You'll probably do well, and if you can convince them to give you a shit job there, you'll be set when you graduate college. You're too straight for rock n' roll."

"I could have told you that," I said with a chuckle. "I liked it much more than I thought I would, though. It made me think."

"Good," David said, coming over to wrap an arm around his wife. "That's all I wanted."

When I got ready to leave a few hours later, I discovered my sister where I least wanted her to be. Mary and Iggy were in the back corner of an unused room, shooting a needle into each other's arms. I didn't say a word. I couldn't. I just turned away, crying.

I went straight to where I'd last seen David, and was lucky enough to find him where I'd left him. I told him everything, and he tore out of the room without a word. Angie and I were hot on his heels, but another musician kept us and everyone else out while David and some other men took care of the situation.

An hour later, David tracked me down. I was crying, wrapped up in some guy's jacket, and drinking whatever Mystic had given me to calm me down. It wasn't working that well.

"She's with a doctor now," he said. His apologetic tone surprised me. "I'm so sorry, love."

"Why are you sorry?" I asked. "You didn't talk her into trying the drugs, did you?"

"No, but I promised you she'd be safe," David pointed out.

"That wasn't a promise I ever expected you to keep," I said. "She wanted to try it ... whatever it was. She made the choice. She is the only one to blame."

"Then, why do I feel so bad?" he asked.

"Because two people you love made a horrible choice," I said. "He may not be your brother, but you love him. I know you do. And we both love her. So, what happens now?"

"What do you mean?" he asked.

"How do I stop her from doing this again?"

"I am the last person you want to ask," he said with a bitter laugh. "I can't stop any of the people I love from screwing up their lives."

I took his hand, and we sat there in silent misery. After a while, I collected my sister and bade my new friends good night.

"Good night, not goodbye?" David asked.

"Not goodbye," I said, kissing his cheek.

During my high school and college days, I spent many nights with punk fans, groupies, and musicians. Some were fun, others terrifying.

My sister kept using drugs until she hit rock bottom and wound up in rehab, just like Iggy. Unlike most of his stints in rehab, hers stuck. Mary has been clean and sober for twenty-five years. She still listens to punk and hard-rock music. She still goes to concerts. She still lives her life to the fullest. She just does it one day at a time now.

I graduated from high school with honors and went to U.C.L.A. I took Lester's advice and got a job as a fact checker for the L.A. Times. When I graduated, I moved to Washington, D.C. to report for the Washington Post.

One night at the Riot House shook my ideals and made me look at things differently. Some changes were subtle, others were sweeping. It was not all positive, but the good outweighed the bad.

A few days ago, I found out that my friend, David, had died. We hadn't spoken in years. I'm sure he barely remembered me, if at all, but he changed the course of my life without trying or knowing that he did anything. That night will forever serve as a reminder that one conversation, one act of kindness, one shared experience, can change the world.

Youth Manifesto Flyer
© Brenda Perlin | BlossomingPress.com

Straight Edge
Jorge P. Newbery
© 2015 – 2016

Jorge P. Newbery founded Upstart Records, which released seven collections from bands such as Stalag 13, Circle One and Red Scare. He crafted Youth Manifesto, a cassette magazine featuring Black Flag, Bad Religion among others, and also promoted gigs throughout Southern California.

My punk friends felt like society's outcasts. They were from all over Southern California, coming from many different schools, and were mostly in their teens and early twenties. All my life, I had been a loner and felt like I did not fit in; however, now, I feel that I did belong. Although my punk friends were mostly white, middle class, and "privileged", they were often tormented. Some were ignored by their parents, gay, abused, or, like me, just didn't conform to society's mold. We had trouble doing what was expected of us and yearned to find a better way to build a better world. For some, alcohol and drugs filled a void and helped dull whatever pained them. For others, the substances helped them feel accepted.

Me and a few others saw what excessive alcohol and drugs were doing to our friends and opted not to partake. This became the straight edge movement, popularized by Washington D.C.'s Minor Threat, which featured a clear-headed lifestyle punctuated by no alcohol, no drugs, and no indiscriminate sex. Suddenly, nerds like me were cool. The punk scene afforded me the first group of solid friends I ever had.

The Clash, Chateau Neuf, Oslo, Norway
by Helge Øverås
Picture Credit: Wikimedia Commons

An Ice Cream Calling: at The Clash Show Asbury Park Convention Hall
1982
Alan Wynzel
© 2016

Alan Wynzel has been chasing him dream of "making it" as a writer for a long time and hasn't given up yet. His childhood memoir, When I Was German, is available on Amazon. Alan lives in northern New Jersey and enjoys spending time with his teenaged children.

In 1982, I was a senior in High School and thought I was Punk. I wasn't, but I really didn't know what Punk was. There weren't any Punk kids in my suburban New

Jersey school, at least not by sight. I was just getting into music, and it was mostly the Doors, Who and Zep, and all that Classic Rock crap (although I still like the Doors, the Stones, and Aerosmith, the rest are crap to me now). At the time, I mostly followed my best friend Andrew's musical taste, which was quite advanced. His father had hundreds of rock records, and he had been playing them for Andrew since he was little. My parents had a few records, mostly classical. My old man liked Bolero; recalling my mother's comments, it apparently gave him wood. My mother listened to AM radio in the kitchen. Seventies Pop and Easy Listening droned in the background while she cooked. So I knew nothing of music. In a used record shop, Andrew picked up a copy of Aerosmith's "Rocks" album, and I, having no clue what I should get, bought a copy for myself.

I did have the good fortune of buying, just by chance, one of the greatest albums of all time: "London Calling" by the Clash. Of course, The Clash were all over the radio during those days. They had made it. So it was my Clash album, my black parachute pants, and my skin tight Members Only lycra demi-sleeve shirts that made me think I was Punk. I was buying my clothes at the Just Shirts store at the mall. What they were selling, really, was New Wave. And my Capezio shoes sealed that deal: I was really a New Waver. I was incredibly naive then. But the girls liked my look and thought I was cool.

I'm lucky there weren't any real Punks at school because they would have stomped my poser ass.

Oi.

I really loved The Clash. I played "London Calling" almost every day. Andrew was into them, too. When we heard The Clash would be playing in Asbury Park at the end of May, we raced down to the mall in my '74 Pontiac LeMans—it managed to start and run that day—to get tickets at the Ticketmaster outlet. We scored a pair and spent the next several weeks in a state of fitful anticipation.

And my coolness with the girls was sealed airtight.

Now, I may have been naive with music, and with Punk, but in other areas I was spot on for eighteen. And Andrew was not. I was dating girls and getting laid, for instance. Also, I was drinking, going to parties, smoking reefers, and trying a few other things. I even had a fake I.D., gotten out of frustration. When I was sixteen, the drinking age in Jersey was still eighteen. But M.A.D.D. was really putting the pressure on the politicians, and it was raised to nineteen, but with grandfathering for the next two years of eighteen year-olds. Which meant I would be able to drink when I was eighteen. But it never came to be, because the age was raised again when I was seventeen to twenty one, and no grandfathering. So I was screwed. But not for long. I gave a friend a case of Heineken to borrow his driver's license (they still issued them without pictures then) and his birth certificate, and went to the courthouse and got myself a County I.D., which worked fine in all the bars and liquor stores.

I had some balls then. Now, I'm not so sure. I'm hoping the statute of limitations has run out on my little crime. Nowadays, I'm sure it would be a felony.

To tell the truth, although it was incredibly cool having a fake I.D., having a car was a real pain in the ass. It made me popular, but mostly with assholes who needed rides or wanted me to buy beer for them.

The long-awaited day finally came and the poser Punk, with his musically-advanced and socially-impaired sidekick, set off in the late afternoon for Asbury Park. But not before I broadcasted the fact to all the chicks in school that were within earshot, and not without praying that my piece of shit Pontiac would make it down the shore and back. (In Jersey, by the way, you don't "go to the beach", you go "down the shore.")

I was well-equipped for the trip. My party inventory was not as extensive as Hunter S. Thompson's in "Fear and Loathing", but it was more than adequate. In the trunk, there were two six-packs of sixteen ounce Budweiser "tall boys" and a pint of blackberry brandy. And secreted in my pocket were a handful of Tylenol with Codeine.

Yes, I was mildly insane.

The beers were standard fare, but I wanted something extra special for the occasion, so I picked up the brandy. A few years later, I would awaken in my Rutgers apartment, my head ringing, my guts churning and my right hand wrapped in a crude, blood-soaked bandage, and vaguely recall how I had put it through a window the night before. And that I had done shots of blackberry brandy at the bar. And then, it all came back to me: the Clash concert and the other windows I had put my fist through, and how each time, I had been drinking blackberry brandy.

And they made a big deal over Angel Dust.

As for the Tylenol with Codeine: I had a case of Mono a few months before. It was really bad; I lost fifteen pounds, spent four days in the hospital and missed two weeks of school. The doctor prescribed the Tylenol because my throat was so swollen and God-awful painful. I couldn't even drink water, which is how I wound up in the hospital, from dehydration.

I had cleverly saved a few pills.

Frankly, I probably wasn't even supposed to be drinking. I remember the doctor said no alcohol for six months after the Mono. That was in January. I went back to drinking in March, I think. Seven Rhinegold tall boys that first time, if I remember correctly. The aluminum cans were so soft. Once emptied, I tore holes in them with my teeth. It was my first time drinking after a painful two-month on the wagon, so...

Understand that I didn't plan on drinking all those beers, and brandy, and popping all those pills myself. I expected to share them. And not much with Andrew; he was a lightweight. I figured we'd meet some girls and what better way to attract teenage girls than with free drinks? (Works well with women of all ages, I have since discovered. Except that now, when my money runs out, they leave.) But we had more going for us than drinks. We were good-looking guys, overall, and then, there was my cool Punk look, enhanced this evening with my black and yellow sleeveless striped fuzzy shirt one of my asshole friends called the "Bumblebee Shirt", along with my gray Member's Only bomber jacket. Plus, I had a car. The fact that it didn't run half the time didn't matter.

What mattered was that it was my own little motel on wheels.

The LeMans made the trip and by early evening, with the sun just about to set, I swerved into a parking spot on one of the four sides of a square park right by the Convention Center. The boardwalk and the ocean were off to our left. The scene was one huge tailgate party, right out in the street. Asbury Park had gone bad long before, and the cops had enough on their hands with murder, rape, and armed robbery. They couldn't be bothered with a bunch of minors drinking in public.

And then, I saw my first Punks. Real ones. Six of them swaggered past in their thick-soled boots, multiple piercings, (with safety pins!!) ripped black jeans and shredded concert-tees. And Mohawks. Huge, solid, spiked Mohawks atop their pale skulls. Guzzling bottles of beer and cursing defiantly. One glanced at me and sneered. I shrank against the side of my car.

Fortunately, they kept on. Andrew had disappeared. It was not until a few moments had passed that he peered out from behind a nearby tree. He tiptoed over.

"Punks," he whispered. "Those were real Punks."

"Yeah," I said. I cracked open a Bud and regarded my reflection in the car window.

"The bumble-bee shirt has to go, man," I said.

It wasn't long before a pair of really cute girls wandered near, and I was able to lure them over by offering them some beers. They weren't Punk or New Wave, just some fairly normal, and safe, Preppie types. But really cute. And they got cuter beer by beer. I laid claim to the better of the two (hey, I drove and bought the damn alcohol, I told Andrew, so I got first pick) who, in addition to her satiny, flowing blonde locks and smooth, silky golden skin, had tits like a stripper.

Ah, but Dear Reader ... beer, brandy, Codeine ... you know where this is headed. No, sadly, I was not destined to get my hands on those beauties that night.

A few hours passed and the show was due to start soon. I'd had about five beers (remember these were sixteen ouncers) and half a pint of brandy by then. And I had impulsively, and discreetly, popped a Codeine not long before. I was flying high. I was buzzed. I was happy.

For a minute, anyway.

We were all leaning against the side of my car, the girls in the middle and Andrew and I on the ends. I was chatting up Melanie Melons. Andrew, who happened to be uncharacteristically garrulous from his beer-and-a-half, seemed to be making progress with Second Best, but still not shabby.

It was time to make my Move.

At that point, however, everything got fuzzy.

I remember either lunging, or falling, or something, against Melanie. Whatever I did, it wasn't received well, because the next thing I knew, the girls were gone. Gone!

And I was on a different plane, man. I had been reconfigured, and my mind and body no longer recognized the standard measures of Space, Time, or Logic.

"Where they go?" I asked Andrew.

"They left, man."

"Why they go?"

"You attacked that girl."

"I did?"

"Well, sort of. You slobbered all over her."

"Oh. I like big boobs. I'm sorry."

"It's okay. It's almost time for the show. Hey, man, maybe you need some fresh salt air. Let's go down by the water. The boardwalk is right over there."

"Okay."

Andrew led me across the street and up the ramp to the boardwalk. Funny thing is, we zig-zagged all the way. It was so funny I giggled.

"What's so funny?"

"We don't walk straight."

The boardwalk was crowded with Punks, Preppies, New Wavers, kids, child molesters, homeless old ladies and down-and-out Asbury Park mole people. And all of them drunk or otherwise wasted. But all I saw was a blur of heads, torsos and limbs that really didn't register with me.

But what I did see clearly was ICE CREAM.

So cried out the big sign atop the ice cream kiosk.

"I wanna ice cream," I said.

"What?"

"Ice cream, man, ice cream, I wanna ice cream, gemme an ice cream, man, please?"

"Uh, Okay."

"I wanna ice cream, NOW! Gemme a fuckin ice cream, NOW!"

"Okay! Shh, quiet, Al, there's some cops over there. Just shhh, I'll get you an ice cream."

Andrew pushed me onto a bench overlooking the sand and the gray, slowly breaking waves. I smelled salt and decay.

"What flavor?"

"What?"

"What flavor ice cream?"

"VANILLA, OF COURSE, IT'S THE BEST FLAVOR. WHAT THE FUCK ELSE WOULD I GET?"

"Okay, okay! Shh, shh, quiet! Be quiet and stay here while I get a cone."

"Okay."

Andrew ran off.

Surf beach, clouds, seagulls, tits, Clash, Pontiac, boardwalk, trash, rusty nails in the planks...

"Here's your ice cream, man."

Andrew handed me a dark brown sugar cone topped with a big globe of vanilla.

"Thanks, man."

Then a fog rolled in. But not from the ocean. From the edges of my brain.

I never ate that ice cream. Instead, I slowly, slowly leaned forward, falling into the fog, and the ice cream slipped from the cone and hit the deck with a splat.

"Oh, no," said Andrew.

"My ice cream."

At this point I began to vomit.

Andrew, apparently discomforted by the impropriety of my actions, pulled me to my feet and began dragging me away. Had he allowed me to remain leaned over on the bench, I would have puked harmlessly on the boardwalk. But erect, it went all down the front of my jacket.

"Come on, let's get back to the car."

"Wanna go the concert. Wanna see Clash."

Some Punks shambled past, laughing.

"London calling!" I shouted at them.

"Come on, let's go."

"London calling! No, Ice Cream calling."

"Shut up. And stop walking like Frankenstein."

"Ice cream calling in da farway town, battle come down, nukeleer riot, ICE CREAM CALLING, FARWAY DOWN, BATTLES GO DOWN!"

"Oh, my God, shhh!"

Andrew opened the door of my car and shoved me in the back seat. It was dark out now.

And darker for me. I blacked out at that point.

When I came to, I thought I was in the middle of a riot. People charging past, screams, bottles breaking, horns blaring, sirens, maddened red faces passing in the glare of the streetlights.

I sat up. Ugh. I stank like puke.

Andrew appeared a few moments later, just as I was thinking, sonofabitch, that idiot left me alone in the car, and I could have choked on my own puke, and died like Jimi Hendrix. And ten years younger and not even knowing how to play guitar.

Andrew appeared to have gone insane. He must have bought a Clash concert tee, and somehow, gotten it ripped to shreds.

"WOOOOOO! It was CRAZY!!! Beer bottles flying, slam dancing, fights, fireworks, fires, it was insane!"

"How was the Clash?"

"Oh, man, you missed the greatest concert of all time!"

"Shut up. I wanna go home. Are you okay to drive?"

"Yeah, no problem."

Andrew calmed down, got serious, and took the wheel. I spider-crawled up front.

But he couldn't start the car. You had to feather the gas pedal just right, and despite my coaching, he just couldn't do it.

"Forget it, I'll drive," I said.

"You're not still wasted?"

"I think I puked it all out."

I managed to start the car, and it stayed running all the way home. And I had lied to Andrew; I was still really wasted. But I managed. It was probably two in the morning when I collapsed in my bed. The next day my mother yelled at me because my jacket smelled like puke and what was I doing at that concert getting so drunk that I threw up?

"No, Ma, I got sick from bad ice cream."

She didn't believe me. But she cleaned that jacket and got the stink out of it.

I wore it for a few more years, through most of college, even though I had decided I didn't want to be a Punk anymore. Faux, or real. But I liked the jacket.

So that's my story. Of how I missed seeing The Clash, didn't get laid, and puked all over myself.

It's been thirty-plus years since then and what did I learn? Well, I still drink. Just no more blackberry brandy, of course. In fact, I'm having some drinks right now. If I take any prescription painkillers, it's for my bad back. As for The Clash—I'm listening to "London Calling" as I write this. I may have missed the concert, but it doesn't matter, it's still one of the best albums ever made. And it's there for me to listen to anytime I want.

It's hard to decide, but I think my favorite song is "Death or Glory."

Or maybe, "The Card Cheat."

What's yours?

As for ice cream, well, it constipates me nowadays, so I eat Soy Dream, instead. Vanilla, of course.

What the fuck else would I get?

Sid Vicious
by Chicao Art Department c/o L. Schorr
Picture Credit: Wikimedia Commons

Sid
Jim Kavanagh
© 2016

Jim Kavanagh owns a small Construction firm in New York City. When he is not working for Fortune 500 companies, he spends time with his sons. He is a stout conservationist who is dedicated to saving the Big Cats. Forever a punk, Jim ran in the streets of NYC from 1977-1981 and lived the "no future" political movement of the times.

I recall the stench of urine when I slowly climbed up the stairs from the E train subway stop at West 4th Street in New York City. Partially hungover and tired, the news was already old about Nancy's death and Sid being to blame.

It's easy to look back and say that it was only a matter of time before Sid followed, and most of the Beatnik writers for the Village Voice and Rolling Stone Magazine had already given Punk Rock, and its following, an epitaph.

After an unsuccessful Sex Pistols American tour, these fucking cum towel writers reveled in his death. They compared punk from "Garbage Pail Kids" to "awful three-chord bands that should all disappear through the gates of the Chelsea".

Years later, after MTV's success and New Wave's connection to Punk, every music writer became experts in the roots of it all.

And the debate began along with the fashion and, eventually, social acceptance.

As an individual who was part of the tribe from that time, I'm not sure what makes me angriest. The people who claimed to have been part of the scene or those who took credit for being the biographers of New York City's punk uprising as it happened.

What went down during that time flew over the heads of so-called music historians. Forty years later, they are still looking up and wondering what really happened.

New York City was the epicenter of Punk in the USA. This leads to many debates. But call it what you will, there is no doubting it. The royal celebrity following and history is undeniable.

Unlike other cities, Punk in NYC not only included music and our "homemade" look, but it also included a political uprising and a street meaning defined by the music itself.

Cities like Boston and Philly had their followings, as well as the entire West Coast, and it's also my opinion that LA's punk influence eventually defined another all-American genre – Grunge!

In all honesty, Sid's death was a real fucking surprise to many. What was never documented was the anger caused by the death. Tears were few in a full-time life of anarchy and political statements against an unjust establishment. It magnified the events of the day and gave us an excuse to act out about everything.

At the same time, other music stepped up to share the platform the Pistols helped define. Some of these followings came with such a large fan base that they couldn't give a crap about Sid's death. New York City had all these types, and it depended in which part of town you hung out. The thrashers (skate board punks, of which I was one), were chameleons. They would adapt to any feelings or punk sound of the area.

If we could successfully sell whatever drugs we were hawking, that is.

It still mystifies me that people today even give a shit about our era. I have found that outside of fashion and music and made-up totally bullshit stories, authentic Punk has long been dead. What's left is Punk music.

Over the years, I have lived with such shame about my contribution to the Punk establishment and people I called friends. I was a true Punk prostitute. A self-serving pig who provided the support of a habit to sustain his own.

Oh, so skillfully, too....

I laughed when William (Idol) Broad's biography and follow-up schmaltzy CD "Kings and Queens" was finally released. It's a William Broad album in my opinion. It tells the story of Billy Idol, but has no raw intensity his other releases have. And the book, impressed he did all the writing, but it's the "Rated G" version of truth he decided to publish. I don't blame him for wanting to change the history...

To soften it a little because of the musical contribution today is amazing: but where it came from is not Punk, no matter what city you picked up on Punk, its roots reek of drugs and death.

I remember Billy Idol asking me what I did (to earn a living) at the Peppermint Lounge one night before we scored "Crazy Eddie and Red Tape" (popular brands of heroin and coke). I told him I worked construction. Small talk before the score – like every Junkie.

Once it's in your hands, you disappear and maybe pop back up later. Wow, those thoughts still hurt me. The control that shit had over us. I always admired Idol's first album because he captured so much of that pain. To this day, his words and feelings reach me.

The only thing that was ever going to lead me out of the life of a chemically addicted punk was construction, prison – or death.

As for Idol, he was great for the New York City punk scene! Straight up! Free tickets and MVP security passes to his local shows. Even a bar tab when he played the Malibu in April of 82.

Idol was always cool about it. But what's worse, there's not a single word about us in his book. And no matter how fucked up Idol got, he could always sing and gave an amazing show. He started an English garage band called Generation X. And has somehow maintained his chops to this day.

Idol in early NYC (1981) was always a quiet guy wearing a beret and prescription sunglasses. His scrawny persona and intelligent charm made you like him from the start.

And heck, here was the lead singer for Generation X – fuck, hanging with us in NYC!

On another note. The idiot historians got it wrong. And I challenge the media who think they know better. In the early days of Idol in NYC, his girl, Perri (the bitch who wanted to go home, because in the UK she was the star) was never ever around. Idol was solo early. And when he was around, with his hair done and not covered with a beret, you knew he was taking the stage somewhere. He had something going on and he included us. Again, not a word in his brain-torched biography.

Then there's the life changer for everyone: Especially, all the needle users at the time. The elephant in the room – Aids!

For the park's celebrities, you never saw so many worlds change – friends, ordinary people (myself included) when Aids was rumored about a year before it became a reality!

Holy crap, I don't think so many people went cold turkey or entered rehab all at the same time throughout the history of drugs in America!

Seriously. We needed to get clean. We became clean quick.

So many died. Even now, I often take a moment to reflect ... such a loss.

And then came MTV. Holy shit, MTV! Idol shot to super stardom, and we all became celebrities in our own right, just because of our look. Village Voice ... Rolling Stone. All decided to talk to us. Jump on a bandwagon they could sell.

Listen. They ALL got it wrong.

No matter what has ever been written, or what stoned celebrities had to say. Nobody got it right. You had to live it. Every day.

And defining it wouldn't be "Punk"!!!

Billy Idol at Vinyl Fetish on Melrose in L.A.
© Brenda Perlin | BlossomingPress.com

No Future
Brenda Perlin
© 2016

Brenda Perlin originates from California and has never left the state. Her books are based upon personal experiences. Brenda is passionate about music and supporting animal rescue programs.

As a teen, I may have had growing pains, insecurities and grievances about not fitting in, but looking back, those punk days were something I treasure the most. It was a time when I was full of passion and a zest for life. Life got tough in my early twenties, but not then.

Most punks complained about being on the streets, not having money and their lousy parents. Some of my friends had it so bad they didn't make it past nineteen. Drug overdoses were rampant and teen suicides were not uncommon.

For me, it was different: Those teen years were golden.

With the exception of the strict rules laid down by my parents, I was free and didn't have to think about the future. I was backing our leaders, the Sex Pistols and their mantra, "NO FUTURE." If I followed that closely enough, I wouldn't have to worry about what came next.

The Who's "Hope I die before I get old" was another one of our mottoes. We were young NOW and that was all that mattered. Everything was a party, a selfish period of playing, listening to music and having a blast.

Some of the finest times took place at Danny's (Okie Dog) in Hollywood. My girlfriends and I ran around as if we were being filmed on reality TV. Gossiping, flirting, taking in the sounds, breathing in the scene. There was a buzz in the air and our nights were as explosive as a stick of dynamite.

One of the biggest eye-openers for me was when I saw Billy Idol and his band at a Vinyl Fetish record store on Melrose in the early eighties. He was there to promote his debut Billy Idol solo album, and I couldn't have been more thrilled. I mean, I was going to see the guy of my dreams, the bleached-haired-god in person. We were revved up. I was so hyped I almost passed out from the excitement, but reality came crashing down after I saw him.

Billy didn't look as heavenly as he did in the videos that played all hours of the day on MTV. No, he looked like a wasted, burnt-out drug addict. That I was not expecting. While standing in front of him, my face blushing a deep crimson, shooting his photo, one shot after the other, he was not in the room. Like Elvis, Billy had left the building. I don't think he was ever there, or would have even remembered being there. He wore a dull expression and didn't make eye-contact. As he took a slow sip of his drink from the small green bottle he held in his left hand, he looked right past me as if I were invisible. I caught a glimpse of his unguarded face, the corners of his mouth drawn downward, the creases around his weathered eyes were just becoming noticeable. He was like a ghost, a shadow of what he once was. Billy reminded me of the Ken Barbie doll – he looked good, but he was actually vacant.

For a young "fangirl", this was something I had not yet faced. Something new. This was a different reality, and it was not appealing. My charmed little protected life was entering another dimension: One of darkness and bleak consequences.

I found peace and serenity on the dirty streets of Hollywood, and Skid Row, to me, was not the ongoing crime scene they showed on TV. For us naïve teens, Skid Row was a playground.

There have been critical reviews for L.A. Punk Rocker not showing the shady side, for not highlighting the dingy underbelly of the times. "I would have liked to hear more about Skid Row and the darker side of life at the time, but I imagine that the decision was made to keep the book fairly upbeat." I mean, if teen rape, suicides and drug addiction are not dark enough then, I don't know what else I could have written.

I didn't face any true hardships first hand because I was blind to the real world and saw it through the lens of my sheltered Valley girl life and the comfort of my home surroundings. At the time, I had few responsibilities and didn't have to concern myself with putting food on the table.

Meeting Billy face-to-face demonstrated that even an icon can fall from grace. Too many wrong steps could cost him everything. Seeing him in that condition reminded me that anyone of us could become an addict, but without his fame and fortune.

The Sex Pistols performing in Trondheim in 1977
Picture Credit: Wikimedia Commons

The Jacket
A Fictional Tale
Mark Barry
© 2016

Mark Barry is an English writer and music fan who has written several novels, including the award-winning The Night Porter. The short stories, King Rocker and One Night In Richmond Park, are featured in the L.A. Punk Rocker anthology. Mark currently resides in Nottingham, England.

Hello there.
I'm a leather jacket. I have a story to tell that you may be interested in. I assume you are interested in punk

rock? You must be to get this far. You may believe what I am about to tell you – if you can suspend disbelief long enough to comprehend that the story is being narrated by a coat – and I hope you do.

This is a true story.

This is a punk story.

Technically speaking, I am a vintage Schott Perfecto leather jacket. That brand is much better known as a Brando. Named after the man who made leather jackets ultra-cool way before Arthur Fonzarelli did. Marlon Brando, in the biker flick, The Wild One.

I'd like to tell you that I knew that particular coat, but I would be fibbing. It was said that James Dean was hardly ever seen without his Perfecto, but I don't know that relative either. It was a big factory and those two relatives were way before my time: It's like you Americans asking a Brit if they know the Queen!

Call me Brando. Or if you're normal, with a healthy degree of skepticism, you can just call me The Jacket.

The Jacket.

That's cool. I'm happy with that.

At the moment, I'm writing to you from a rack in BackSlash, the popular Nottingham vintage clothes shop on the top of Market Street. It's nearly Christmas. Life outside the shop is unseasonably warm. I overheard the sales staff saying that because of El Nino, it's going to be like this for a while.

The rack is opposite the changing rooms round the back of the shop. I hang with twenty other coats and jackets of all kinds, mostly associated with music. I share with the soul boy scarlet Harringtons, the Stax Crombies (and the felt collars); the voluminous Mod Parkas (and the arctic ones, which are completely different entirely); the Pitmen's Donkeys, the Quo Denims (some bleached, some stained and patched, some still smelling slightly of Patchouli), and the sleek, super-shiny, uber-cool Bryan Ferry leather box jackets.

Every time I hang next to one of those, I can almost hear Slave to Love in the stitching.

I've been pretty transient, as you shall see, and it is fair to comment that I have had something of a, ahum, colourful history. Probably wouldn't have been traded or sold so much if people actually knew where I'd been, and who I've seen, (and who actually owned me), but there you go.

My makers, the Schott Family, are originally Russian, but I was made in New York in 1968. In their main factory on Manhattan's Lower East Side. I'm nearly fifty. Jet black (natch), scuffed, scratched, mildly wrinkled, nobbly, nicked, nipped, tucked, dented and bruised, but surprisingly well preserved. There is a five inch slash on the underside of my left arm, which has been stitched (I'll tell you about that later), but you can scarcely see it. Different matter if it were on the upper half. Thank God, I am made of Kansas cowhide. At Schott's, they make coats to last – and I wasn't cheap.

I found my way to Britain sometime in 1975. I was originally owned by an old-school Steppenwolf biker in Minnesota (name of Dave, with a big passion for British metal, like Sabbath and – especially Zep). I can handle music like that, and I would tap my feet to it like a good un – if I had feet that is, which I don't, but it was while I was in Minnesota that I discovered punk and that was that. Dave and I went to see MC5 in Detroit one night in early 1972. In hindsight, they didn't look like punks.

They looked like hippies – I mean, the lead singer, had an afro! – but the speed. The power. The fuck-you attitude. In your face. In your face. They looked like they would jump into the crowd at the first sign of a heckle and kick the fuck out of anything that moved. They were beasts, and I loved every second of that night. I have never forgotten it. The stink, the tobacco smoke (I have a tiny scorch on my bottom belt from that very night), the sheer adrenaline, and the sweat of the mad pogoing and moshing going on around me. It was something else.

Screaming guitars, a drummer who looked as if he was going to pass out through his crazed exertions, and at the front, the lead singer with bad, bad, bad gold teeth – a hybrid of black-power soul singer, west coast hippie and starving mugger, breathing fire and brimstone into your terrified mush.

Kick. Out. The Jams.

I was stunned, as much as a jacket can ever be stunned, and simultaneously hooked. Up to that point, and metaphorically, of course, I used to watch Dave's bands with a polite and slightly jolly smile inside.

Now, after MC5, I was a believer. It was MC5's home town, too, and the crowd went insane, absolutely, completely and totally crackers.

Dave wasn't the type to get excited – at gigs, he used to stand at the back near the bar with a bottle in his hand sipping, watching, analyzing. With his Viking hair and bushy beard, he was an unlikely punk and, truth be told, he only went to see the Detroit funsters because a pal of his got free tickets, and he went back to his British rock shortly afterwards (we saw Sabbath on the Vol 4 tour).

AND, he thought they were rock, but a few journalists on the fringes were calling them a punk band, so you have to forgive him. Me? I knew they were punk the first moment I saw them, even if I was only vaguely aware of what that actually meant, and I was completely addicted to punk rock from that point.

I wish I could speak because I would have asked Dave to go see way more punk bands, but he never did. Just hard rock, which, as I said, is passable in a sort of lukewarm sense.

Like apple pie.

You're never going to get a stinking, brooding, red-hot, vein-pumped, high-voltage, bishop's mitre-headed Eiffel tower of a hard-on for apple pie, but you're not going to refuse a second helping if there's one going begging.

Now, are you?

Somehow or other, I ended up in London's Portobello Road in 1975. I don't fully know how. I've lived in Britain ever since. I love the place and my owners have, by and large, looked after me well. And I've had all the punk rock I could have wanted.

Portobello Road wasn't my home for long, but I got to see hundreds and hundreds of nascent proto-punks while I was there, and sooner or later someone bought me. Turned out he was a punk from Nottingham, called Jeff, one of the first of the lot on his first trip to the markets down in London.

Jeff and me were together for a couple of years and the highlight of that was seeing the Sex Pistols at The Boat Club in Nottingham, on one of the hottest nights of the year in August 1976, in the middle of a summer that was one long desert metaphor.

At the Boat Club, like many small venues, there was no air conditioning, the place was jammed, and I couldn't see a thing, but the Pistols were tight, on fire. Awe inspiring. The Boat had a low ceiling and the roaring guitars, thumping drums and throbbing bass simply could not escape and all of it crashed into itself, a detonation, a paroxysm, an explosion of fire and flame and colour: I felt it in my lining.

The boys played some classics that night, too – Liar, No Feelings and two of my favourite Pistols records – Pretty Vacant, which, for me, was the best punk single ever made. They played Stepping Stone, which is a cover, I know, but they owned it, and I couldn't stop humming it for a week. It's still up there – it really is, with all the other punk anthems. The crowd went crazy in the heat – it was so rammed, no-one could get to the bar and more than one person flaked out in the heat from all that pogoing, and unlike Dave, Jeff pogoed like an excitable kangaroo on speed. It was something special.

Jeff and me were on the scene in Nottingham's Market Square. Every Saturday, the old Square was one big battleground. Punks. Soul Boys. Teds. Rockers and the worst of the lot, the football lads (though they, like a Venn diagram, overlapped with the music tribes). It was like a scene from a film. You would think the locals would be terrified, but no – they wandered past the fighting bodies, sometimes stacked six high, the strongest fighter knee deep in the dead, as it were – as if it was the most normal thing in the world.

Jeff used to get proper stuck in – well, he did until he got fined ten quid for Breach Of The Peace, and he didn't like that at all. He was wearing me at the time. That's how I got the slash. A Mod with a face like Piggy from Lord of the Flies attacked him with a Stanley knife. Up came the arm to defend himself and boom, I was slashed.

Jeff liked me so much, he had me stitched up by a local seamstress, and she did a great job.

Afterwards, Jeff slowly lost interest. Not overnight, but over a period of about a year. Not just hanging around in the Square with the others and going to bands, but in everything. I'm not sure whether it was the court appearance, the attack, or just punk's appeal, but he stopped peroxiding his hair and went straight.

I heard on the jacket grapevine that he became a plumber.

I remember us seeing Siouxsie and the Banshees at the Boat Club later on that year. They were canny – Siouxsie was booked under the name Janet and the Icebergs but luckily for Jeff, he was well connected with the lads at Selectadisc at the time, and they were the first to pick up the real identity of the band about to play, and he got a ticket.

If it were possible, the place was even more packed than when the Pistols visited. Whoever thought the Iceberg ploy was a clever one ought to rethink his marketing strategy – every punk in Nottingham turned up that night and it was one electric gig.

Shortly afterwards, Jeff put me down on a bedful of jackets at a party at a smart house in Papplewick and that was the last I ever saw of him, because I got pinched by a proper scrote called Vince, a Damned fanatic, who lived in Sutton-In-Ashfield, a town twenty miles north of Nottingham. We spent six months together, and it was through him I saw the dark side of punk, the side few people ever talk about. See, Vince was a druggie, primarily (but not completely) a pillhead. Uppers and downers, sometimes the stuff they give horses as an anaesthetic and mostly (because it was cheap, and Vince had never held down a job for more than a week or so) lighter fuel.

Yes, I was stolen by a gas sniffer; someone who used to sit on Sutton Lawn with his mates, sniffing from a tin the size of a small tube of Right Guard (something he seriously needed, much more than the gas).

There he was, my new owner, in the cold of midwinter dark night, on a park bench, giggling, lumps of snot dropping onto his tee shirt, saliva hanging from his lips like aluminum cable, silvered, gas-inspired drooling, eyes leaking.

Vince and me lived in a series of squats. He treated me well, though. I was his most treasured possession, apart from his Zippo lighter and any hair dye he could get hold of. Many a time his punk mates and dealer acquaintances had cast admiring glances my way, but Vince was having none of it.

Vince took an overdose (six months after stealing mc) following a night at the Grey Topper in Jacksdale. It wasn't a particularly good gig, but it may have been The Stranglers, or The UK Subs – but you can sympathise with me after experiencing your owner lying in a malodourous toilet, in some nauseating squat deep in Brown Town, Sutton-in-Ashfield, retching, semi-conscious, bloodshot eyes rolling up into his skull. An ambulance arrived, though, despite the best efforts of a seriously underfunded NHS, Vince died in the night, and I was on the move again.

Vince's mother gave me to a charity shop some weeks later, and I was picked up by a girl called Lisa, an Italian girl who loved her punk and spent every spare moment either planning gigs, attending gigs or buying vinyl from places like Selectadisc, or Virgin Records. We saw a ton of bands together. She had one amazing collection of records.

Lisa worked in a bank and wasn't (relatively) short of money and all of that went on music, clothes, jewellery and travelling to gigs. In the short time I was with her, we saw a ton of punk at places like the Topper, Retford Porterhouse, the magnificently filthy Sandpiper Club. We travelled to Birmingham and up to Sheffield and over to Manchester. It was a great time, but all things come to an end. Lisa was dispatched to a branch in London and with her promotion, she seemed to have her fill of punk, and I found myself where I started, but this time, in Chelsea, and that, ladies and gentlemen, is what makes me special.

I don't mean that in a narcissistic sense. I'm not unique. They spawned a hundred of me a day, at one point, back at Schott's factory. Throw a stick in a seventies shopping mall, and it would connect with a black leather jacket, but one afternoon something happened to me to make me unique, and I am VERY proud of that, thank you very much, and I don't actually give a fuck whether you think I'm a narcissist or not, if a jacket can ever be described like that.

Seriously, I don't. I've been around punks way too long to care what you think of me.

One afternoon, the market stall owner, Daphne, from Barnet, – who was seriously into The Slits, the Spex and the aforementioned Siouxsie, and who could be seen on the market and in the clubs, coal-black hair extending a foot above her head like some Mephisthophelean halo; stick thin, I mean bamboo-stick thin, through way too much booze and speed, and who sometimes covered every inch of her face with ceramic-white stage paint she purloined from a theatre in the West End – was visited by a fashion designer, and she bought me on sight, no haggling, no questions asked. She even gave Daphne a tip, which would go straight up her nose that night, probably at the Marquee, the Palace, the Hope and Anchor.

The fashion designer, who I hardly saw as I was in a giant holdall, took me across London to a warehouse in the East End, and I was thrown into a room along with a ton of other punk clothes. Trousers, Tartan and Bondage, Leather and Jeans. Converse baseball boots, foul smelling gym plimsolls, and Doc Martens, of all different colours. Tee shirts and vests of all kinds emblazoned with all sorts of slogans.

And there were other coats, one or two, like me, who had a similar form of sentience to mine, so I could converse with them, but they were new and didn't have much to say for themselves, so I mostly just waited in the foul-smelling cellar in silence until one day, I saw him.

I couldn't believe it.

My new owner.

This'll faccin do, he said, the first words I ever heard him mutter. Yeh, I like this faccer.

Tall, stripey tee shirt, black tube jeans ripped at the knees, Converse baseball boots.

This fits a treat, Sid Vicious said. I'll wear it now for the trip over. Facc it.

This was 1978, and I became part of the infamous (and some say disastrous) Pistols US Tour.

I appeared on stage with the boys. Imagine that? Not every gig, just the two, in San Antonio and in Tulsa (Sid, bless him, had more than one jacket, and he could pick and choose), but they were enough.

Even though the American fans hated them; by and large, simply didn't get them, being there when the Pistols played Anarchy, Holidays, Feelings and God Save The Queen and, my favourite punk track of all time, Pretty Vacant, was something special. I'll never forget it until the day I am too old and battered to resell, until I end up in landfill.

Unbelievable thrill. The sheer energy and power they could generate, the in-your-face threat, the beating drums, the heads-up, heads-down power chords and the sheer rage and hatred the boys could generate, never ending, even when faced with a wall of indifference (which, let's be honest, only made Johnny worse).

I know Sid couldn't play a note, and he was off his nut most of the time, but that was punk, wasn't it. He LOOKED fantastic, just like a punk should look and that sheer pick-up-a-bass-and-play ethos was exactly what it was about. And he liked me – we gelled. They were great times for me on the road in the southern states of America.

But yet again, it had to end, as it always does.

The boys, perhaps because of the lack of interest and the total lack of respect they received over there, fought even more than usual. They blew up, and I watched it happen. It was heartbreaking from a fan's point of view.

I loved the Pistols, and I still do. No other punk band got close. They were the mother lode for a thousand bands and watching them die in the States was a desolate, melancholy epitaph they didn't deserve.

My role in the Sex Pistols culminated one night in New York. Yes, I was there with Sid and his girlfriend, Nancy, in the Chelsea Hotel.

And I know exactly what happened.

But that's another story. Sorry. Not ready to tell that one yet. Probably dangerous, too, and as I said – I'm looking for the quiet life.

They say the Flower Power era ended with Charlie Manson (who owned one of my brothers, incidentally) and his gang of drooling nutters in Beverly Hills, but when did punk end? That era, the first era. Was it with the demise of Sid and Nancy? Possibly. All great revolutionary epochs end not with a whimper but with violence, blood and death, so that would get my vote.

I mean, with Sid dead, what would be the point of punk rock?

There were other reasons punk faded away. While I was in storage somewhere in London, several things happened to the world outside. One, the election of Thatcher began to bear fruit. A lunatic who saw herself as some political Joan of Arc, but who, I am told, was closer to Pol Pot in temperament, her Year Zero politics sounded the clarion of death for many communities where punk was a lifestyle. Like Jacksdale and its doomed Grey Topper. And Ripley with its famous bandstand. And Calverton … and Mexborough and … and…

The same with Ronald Reagan in the USA, with his trickle-down economic madness and his tiny-dicked anti-Soviet rhetoric that, in 1983, bought the world to the brink of the apocalypse. (The Americans were three minutes and sixteen seconds away from launching a hundred ICBMs at East Germany, something which fills me with shame. AND some of them were about to be launched from the East Anglian region of my adopted homeland, too.)

When you think about it, with lunatics like this at the helm, what is the point of punk? Johnny Rotten, Iggy Pop, Lou Reed, Captain Sensible and the pseudo-vampyrous Dave Vanian are fucking pillars of the community by comparison.

But I digress again – for me (and I feel well qualified to argue this point), the signal for the real death of punk rock was the release of a song called "Is Vic There?" by a Scottish band called Department S.

That song provided the rainbow bridge between the Valhalla of punk rock and the prosaic Midgard of New Romance. The original Top Of The Pops appearance was around – I've watched one of my owners search for Department S on the internet in her bedroom, so I have seen it for myself – and it sounds like punk, it has the punk tempo and some of the punk attitude, but the lead singer is smartly dressed, has a muchas cococobana moustache and a half-perm.

You know, the short back and sides, but topped, like some surreal slab cake, with a permed quiff.

A perm. Seriously. Sid must have been turning in his grave.

Hair like that existed and already, around the markets of Portobello Road, Carnaby Street, Camden and Chelsea, the punks were swapping their Sid jackets for Steve Strange grey overcoats.

While wearing eyeliner.

Don't agree with me that this was important? Well. Think of your own benchmark. What do you want? To be told what to think by a coat? Who do you think killed Bambi?

So Sid died, and I ended up in storage. Alone, and no-one to chat with. I must have spent years there, but I am a jacket so time has zero meaning. It could have been a single second or it could have been an infinity, but when I was released, would you believe I was bought from a charity shop in Finchley by Lisa, the Italian banker from back in the day, who recognised me immediately.

I think she paid a fiver, but she was a different woman then, with kids and a nice house, and I was an impulse buy for her, so she never actually wore me, and I spent time in her attic until finally, when she visited her mum back in Nottingham, I was back on the circuit and eventually, after several owners, I found myself here, on the rack, in BackSlash.

There it is, my new friends.

The somewhat abridged tale of the Brando Jacket. Surprised? Well, I guess you are most surprised that a jacket can narrate! How I am able to do that is my secret (though there was this Wizard Jeff and me met while watching Penetration in Barbarellas), and it shall (more or less) remain that way.

I am old and tired, battered and bruised, a little lacking in lustre. They say you humans look more and more like babies the older you get, as if you are regressing into a natural state, but that doesn't happen with jackets. Oh, no. We look punished. I mean, my lining is starting to unravel and unthread, there are stains and scuffs and rips and weals, and the woman who runs BackSlash (who drives a hard bargain), insists on asking twenty quid for me. No wonder I've been here a while.

At one time, I could be in and out of a vintage shop in hours, almost before the ink has dried on the price tag, but not this time. I've watched all sorts of coats come and go and there I hang, at the back quietly waiting for a new owner, a new experience (but a quiet one, as I said).

Now, I'm a museum piece – the Hard Rock Café would break the bank if they knew who owned me all those years ago in another world.

Behold, burger eaters! Here be Sid Vicious' Brando jacket.

A jacket like me doesn't come with a certificate of authenticity. This is just between you and me.

At night, when the shop is dark and all I can hear is the sound of the Market Street revellers walking up and down underneath the lamplights, a passing car, a double-decker bus, the chiming bell of the new tram coming back and forth, I think about what I saw in the punk era and who I saw. The shop itself comes to life and every now and again, I hear whispers from downstairs in the Ladies and the Gents' shirts; a conversation or two, a moment of stolen gossip amongst the sentient, but mostly, the silence allows me to contemplate punk rock.

I remember the nineties a bit – Manchester, Oasis, House music, Blur, all that Britpop sound – but I cannot remember the past decade at all. Can you?

I mean, Mumford and Sons? What's all that about?

But I can remember punk clearly, as clear as I can hear the sounds of the winter night outside.

Who was my favourite? Well, that's easy, isn't it. The greatest punk band there ever was, is and will be, the Sex Pistols – and I am not saying that just because Sid was my owner. I am saying it because it's true.

No-one had the power, the vivaciousness, the vim, the ironic cheerfulness, the high-spirited, imp-like humour combined with the voltage to pull it all off.

When they were at their best, no-one could touch them. Tight? No-one was tighter than Matlock, Cookie and Jones. I was on stage when they played Stepping Stone in Tulsa, and I saw them play it in Nottingham all those halcyon years ago. Incredible. It's a question of perception – something you get quite a lot of, being a jacket. In there pitching. Watching from a distance. Two ways of looking at the same thing and somehow, it all means the same.

There were other bands I loved and had the honour to see – The Ruts for one, with Babylon's Burning, which is up there. The Stranglers, who, if I'm being honest, were an acquired taste, ditto The Clash, who everyone loved, even more than the Pistols, but I have never been convinced. Way too self-conscious and knowing. Generation X and King Rocker. Siouxsie, X-Ray Spex with Germ Free Adolescent, and The Slits, who could be proper ramshackle – I saw those at the Porterhouse. Rubbish, but they had a certain charm. Then Buzzcocks, who, another biker jacket told me a couple of weeks ago, are still going strong, like Idol. Ever Fallen In Love. The best pop song ever recorded? I saw them play that in Manchester. Can't take a memory like that away. Then, in the early days, I saw now-forgotten bands like Eater, and Chelsea and Penetration and Slaughter and the Dogs and in the latter days, I was there when the UK Subs and Comsat Angels, and the messengers of Oi appeared, like Cockney Rejects, the sons of Sham 69 who imploded amidst a torrent of fists and boots on the dance-floor as grudges spawned on the blood-spattered terraces, enmeshed with the hatred of the National Front, spilled into the clubs.

I saw local bands like Some Chicken. American bands like Iggy, Talking Heads, and Richard Hell, and the Voidoids, and I was at parties when I heard Undertones, The Vapors, Skids, Split Enz, XTC, The Creatures and Blondie (always loved Debs – which was it for you? Debbie Harry or Kate Bush?), and The Members' Sound Of The Suburbs, and Plasmatics, and Rubinoos, and Joe Jackson, and the wonderfully named Vibrators, and Eddie and The Hot Rods, and Dr Feelgood, and The Damned, and Iggy and the original US punk influence of Lou Reed, and Velvet Underground, and the Cramps and one of my very, very favourites, Jilted John. Singers of my favourite punk-pop song – like the Monkees in tartan bondage trousers.

I've been going out with a girl … her name is JooOOLie…

I was there when punk got political with Sandinista and Jona Lewie's Stop the Cavalry, and I remember Lisa saying to her mate in the Coffee Pot in Arnold that the New Musical Express was more like a statement for the Socialist Workers Party (with writers like Burchill and Penman, and Steven Wells, and future arts guru and megastar Paul Morley, who Lisa loved and had a big crush on).

I was somewhere about when the Nottingham Virgin Records store was taken to court for plastering its windows with Never Mind The Bollocks marketing material (and John Mortimer of Rumpole of the Bailey fame defended it to the end).

And I was there, as I mentioned briefly, when Sid took his final breath and with him went – in some legends, in some myth – the spirit of punk rock.

So, even though I hang here, in a vintage shop in the middle of an unremarkable Midlands town, unwanted, unloved, unmourned, alone, and faintly smelling of thirty years of musical history, I was there at the birth of punk, and I was there at its death.

There was a hoodie here a few weeks ago. A brand I didn't recognise. It, like me, was sentient, and we conversed. He was once owned by a rapper, a Grime rapper, or something, the British hiphop version of the American stuff, he said, and as you probably know, the rap boys tend to swap clothes regularly. The big boys buy a new pair of expensive trainers every day, apparently.

When I told him who I was and where I'd been, he said to me, man, you are one motherfucker of a jacket.

I would have blushed, had I possessed a face, which I don't. But yes, when I think about this, I realise that what he said was true.

To be there at the beginning of something magical like punk, and to stay with it to the end, was something special.

It does make me one, ahum, motherfucker of a jacket.

A young man takes me to the light and looks at me. He wears fashionable spectacles and has a hipster beard, like they all do now. He has a Quadrophenia tee shirt, and he wears a little too much aftershave. He tries me on. I fit him perfectly. He calls his friend on his mobile telephone. He takes a selfie in the mirror and then sends the photograph through the internet. He stands there for a second and then, I hear a beep. The young man grins, takes me off and walks me to the counter. There is no haggling in BackSlash, so he pays the twenty pounds on a card, and I am placed in a shopping bag and soon, once more, I am out in the world, my last ride and pretty vacant.

Makeup artist Christian Saavedra with Brenda Perlin
© Brenda Perlin | BlossomingPress.com

The Mirror
Brenda Perlin
© 2016

"Are you ready to see yourself in the mirror?" Christian asked after applying David Bowie's Aladdin Sane's lightning bolt makeup.

Upon hearing those words, I became emotional, almost to tears, as I sheepishly strolled over to the mirror.

At that moment, the experience was almost spiritual. Having my face painted like Bowie reminded me of the man and his contributions. I was no longer looking at myself, but someone who was privileged to have lived in the same world as this legend. And it wasn't just his music that was inspiring. He showed us that we could be whoever we wished to be and made it okay to different.

As I peered in the mirror, I beamed with pride and, somehow, felt closer to our American Idol.

Social Distortion, Mr. Mike Ness 12/19/82 Lazaro's Ballroom.
Jorge Newberry and Alison Braun promoted this show.
© Alison Braun Photography

David Bowie Paramount Theater Seattle, WA 12/20/1991
Photo by Alison Braun — at Seattle
© Alison Braun Photography

UK Subs 5/2/1986 Fenders ballroom
© Alison Braun Photography

Adolescents at Fenders Ballroom November 19,1986
© Alison Braun Photography

Biafra and Zappa at an anti censorship event in L.A.
© Alison Braun Photography

Vice Squad 8/18/1982 Florentine Gardens
© Alison Braun Photography

Keith Morris, Circle Jerks. Whisky, 1981
© Alison Braun Photography

Rollins first Gig with Black Flag. Aug 1981
© Alison Braun Photography

Joey Ramone — with Ramones
© Alison Braun Photography

Billy Idol at House of Blues in Las Vegas, 2016
© Brenda Perlin | BlossomingPress.com

Billy Idol at House of Blues in Las Vegas, 2016
© Brenda Perlin | BlossomingPress.com

Billy Idol at House of Blues in Las Vegas, 2016
© Brenda Perlin | BlossomingPress.com

Image by Silvano L. Marlon
© Brenda Perlin | BlossomingPress.com

Wikimedia Commons Picture Credits:

"The Thin White Duke 76" by Jean-Luc Ourlin
Uploaded by Auréola.
Originally posted to Flickr as David Bowie.
Licensed under CC BY-SA 2.0 via Wikimedia Commons
https://commons.wikimedia.org/wiki/File:The_Thin_White_Duke_76.jpg#/media/File:The_Thin_White_Duke_76.jpg

Image: Scott Weiland Live at Pepsi Music Stadium
April 16 2007
This image was originally posted to Flickr by Edvill at
http://flickr.com/photos/84766178@N00/477495018
https://it.wikipedia.org/wiki/File:Scott_weiland!.jpg
https://commons.wikimedia.org/wiki/File:Scott_weiland%21.jpg

Iggy-Pop 1977" by Michael Markos.
Licensed under CC BY-SA 2.0 via Wikimedia Commons
https://commons.wikimedia.org/wiki/File:Iggy-Pop_1977.jpg#/media/File:Iggy-Pop_1977.jpg

Adapted from the Wikimedia Commons file
Image: The Clash, Chateau Neuf, Oslo, Norway by Helge Øverås
https://commons.wikimedia.org/wiki/File:Clash_21051980_12_800.jpg

Adapted from the Wikimedia Commons file
Image: Vicious.jpg by Chicao Art Department c/o L. Schorr
https://commons.wikimedia.org/wiki/File:Vicious.jpg

Adapted from the Wikimedia Commons file
Image The Sex Pistols performing in Trondheim in 1977 (Sid Vicious left, Steve Jones center, and Johnny Rotten right)
Riksarkivet (National Archives of Norway) Photograph: Billedbladet NÅ/Arne S. Nielsen
https://commons.wikimedia.org/wiki/File:SexPistolsNorway1977.jpg

THANK YOU FOR READING PUNK ROCKER

Hope you enjoyed going back in time with me and my friends. I would love to hear from you. Do you mind sharing this with people you know or post a review on Amazon? Your feedback is so helpful.

I appreciate you taking the time to read Punk Rocker.

Brenda Perlin

CPSIA information can be obtained
at www.ICGtesting.com
Printed in the USA
LVHW081515270519
619177LV00041B/1700/P

9 781523 806676